Book Five

EPIC ZERO 5

Tales of an Unlikely Kid Outlaw

By

R.L. Ullman

But That's
Another Story...
Press

Cover design and illustrations by Yusup Mediyan

Published by But That's Another Story… Press
Ridgefield, CT

Printed in the United States of America.

First Printing, 2019.

ISBN: 978-0-9984129-6-2
Library of Congress Control Number: 2019903548

For Stan,
who filled my mind with magic

BOOKS BY R.L. ULLMAN

EPIC ZERO SERIES

EPIC ZERO:
Tales of a Not-So-Super 6th Grader

EPIC ZERO Extra:
FREE at rlullman.com

EPIC ZERO 2:
Tales of a Pathetic Power Failure

EPIC ZERO 3:
Tales of a Super Lame Last Hope

EPIC ZERO 4:
Tales of a Total Waste of Time

EPIC ZERO 5:
Tales of an Unlikely Kid Outlaw

EPIC ZERO 6:
Tales of a Major Meta Disaster

EPIC ZERO 7:
Tales of a Long Lost Leader

MONSTER PROBLEMS SERIES

MONSTER PROBLEMS:
Vampire Misfire

MONSTER PROBLEMS 2:
Down for the Count

MONSTER PROBLEMS 3:
Prince of Dorkness

TABLE OF CONTENTS

ONE

I GET ROCKED

I'm running through a subway tunnel in hot pursuit.

My prey this time are a brother-sister Meta villain team called Mover and Shaker. Apparently, they broke into the Keystone City Museum and walked out with millions of dollars in precious gemstones. Then, they made their escape through the subway system.

It was a great plan, but unfortunately for them, they're not the only brother-sister Meta team down here.

"Can you possibly move any slower?" Grace barks, zipping over my head with a flashlight in hand. "They're getting away!"

Of course, they're probably the more united brother-sister Meta team down here.

"I'm going as fast as I can," I call out, my voice

echoing through the tunnel. But deep down I realize she's right. Maybe I am dogging it a little. After all, I've barely worked up a sweat.

I mean, normally I'm geeked up for a chance to wrangle up some rogues. But right now, I'm feeling a little cautious. Maybe I should explain.

Up until about ten minutes ago, Grace and I were stuck on the Waystation doing homework while the rest of the team was out on a mission. So, I pretty much resigned myself to an evening of algebra and ice cream.

That is, until the Meta Monitor started blaring.

Even though our parents told us to stay put no matter what, they couldn't really expect us to ignore the alarm, could they? I mean, we're superheroes for Pete's sake. Sometimes you need to sacrifice math to save the day!

I was thinking this would be awesome.

Then, I found out the crooks went underground.

That's when things got a little less awesome.

You see, if there's one thing I hate, it's going underground. And it's not because I'm afraid of the dark. Trust me, I moved past that stage years ago (and no, nightlights don't count). And it's definitely not because I get claustrophobic. I've been in plenty of tight spots before and managed to hold my own.

So, what's my beef with going underground?

Well, in my experience, nothing—and I mean NOTHING—good ever happens underground.

Take Meta-Taker for instance. The first time I laid eyes on that monster was when he popped out of the hole the Worm dug for him. Then there was my nightmare encounter with Alligazer in the sewer system.

See the pattern here?

Yet, where do I find myself now?

Running through Keystone City's subway system— underground.

Yep, you'd think I'd have learned by now.

Of course, I could have opted out. In fact, I pretty much convinced myself I wouldn't be going on this little subterranean adventure. Then Grace called me a 'chicken.'

So that pretty much explains what I'm doing here.

"Come on, slowpoke!" Grace yells, flying around the bend. "You should rename yourself Molasses Boy!"

Well, that was rude. But when I shine my flashlight in her direction she's already gone. Man, I sure wish I had her confidence right now. But I guess I've been burned too many times underground before.

Nevertheless, I pick up the pace. Other than Grace's barbs, the only sounds I hear are my footsteps sloshing through puddles and my heart beating way too fast.

Sometimes I can't believe I'm doing this stuff.

In retrospect, I guess I could have copied Grace's flight power. After all, running through a subway tunnel is risky business. In particular, you want to avoid the third rail. That's the one that supplies power to the train's electric motor. One accidental touch could fry you to a crisp.

So that's pretty unnerving.

Speaking of unnerving, I barely had time to read the profiles of Mover and Shaker before we got here. What I did catch is that Mover and Shaker are Meta-morphs who can change their molecular structures into stone and sand, respectively. I suppose if their criminal careers don't work out, they could open a half-way decent landscaping business.

I flash my light along the walls. Boy, it's depressing down here. Everywhere I look is gray concrete and black mold. Yuck! The sooner we get out of here the better.

The problem is that I'm not even sure we're going the right way. Grace picked this direction and I wasn't going to argue with her, but the subway system is massive. We've probably been heading down this tunnel for five minutes without finding any—

"AHHH!"

That scream!

It's Grace!

Without thinking, I sprint towards her voice, shining my flashlight everywhere but I don't see her. After about fifty yards I stop and catch my breath.

Where the heck is she?

Suddenly, my flashlight is knocked out of my hand and I hear it CLANKING onto the rails.

Great. It's pitch dark and someone is next to me!

Did I mention I hate going underground?

"Well, well," comes a female voice, echoing through the tunnel. "We must be the Pied Pipers for Meta children because it seems like we're being followed by all of these annoying costumed kids."

I reach into my utility belt and activate my flare. It lights up like a sparkler and I suddenly find myself face-to-face with a woman. But she's no ordinary woman.

My jaw drops as I watch her features shift around on her face—her left eye moving to where her nose should be, and her nose moving up to her forehead. For a second, I think I'm going to be sick, and then I remember I'm staring at Shaker, whose entire body is made of sand.

"Where's Glory Girl?" I demand.

"Right here, kid," comes a deep, gravelly voice.

I spin around to find a massive pile of rocks standing behind me. It's Mover—and he's holding Grace! I crane my neck to take him all in because he's at least seven feet tall with muscles the size of boulders.

Then, I realize he's standing right on the third rail—with Grace in his arms! But why isn't there any crazy electricity? Then it hits me. He's all rock, so he's grounded—the electricity can't affect him. But if he drops Grace, she'll be electrocuted!

"Take it easy, rockhead," I say. "Or you'll be sorry."

Laughter echoes through the tunnel.

"Well, I didn't think it was funny," I mutter.

"You're cute, kid," Shaker says, her body shifting

from the shape of a woman into the shape of a giant hammer. "But we've got places to go. So, I think it's time to pound sand."

Um, what?

Then, she swings down at me!

I dive out of the way before—

BOOM!

Dirt and steel explode all around me. I look back to find a giant hole right where I was standing. Wow, she completely smashed through the rails!

That was close, but with Grace down for the count, it's all up to me. Luckily, I've got some tricks of my own.

But just as I'm about to negate their powers, there's a RUMBLING behind me, and my legs start shaking.

I wheel around to see two lights heading our way, growing larger by the second. Uh-oh. Those are headlights. Which means… a subway train is coming!

"Catch, kid," Mover says, throwing Grace at me.

I catch her, but she's so heavy I tumble backward. I hit the tracks hard but squeeze Grace tight, preventing her from rolling onto the third rail.

Then, Mover throws a large sack over his shoulder and jumps, busting through the thick, concrete ceiling. I shield Grace with my body as chunks of debris crash down onto the tracks.

"Sorry, kid," Shaker says, grabbing a sack of her own. "But you two picked a really crummy way to die."

Then, she morphs her body into a spring and

bounces out of the tunnel.

No! They're getting away!

SCCRREEEEECCCCHHHH!

The train!

It's braking, but it's coming in too fast!

I'm about to copy Grace's powers and fly us out of here when I notice the hole in the tracks. When the subway reaches it, it'll derail the train and injure all of those people!

I've got seconds to do something. But what?

Then, I notice sand particles on the ground.

Shaker's particles! That's right! Her Meta profile said she loses sand particles from her body, but they always find their way back to her!

That's it!

I put my palm over the sand and concentrate hard, activating my duplication powers.

But when I look up, the train is nearly on top of us!

I need to time this perfectly!

I concentrate hard and then watch in amazement as my right arm turns to pure sand. Boy, that's itchy, but there's no time to scratch. Instead, I encase Grace inside my sandy appendage and then push it out of the tunnel like a water plume, sending Grace to safety.

One job done, one left to do.

HOOONNNKKK!

It's here!

I look up and meet the terrified eyes of the subway

driver, whose handlebar mustache is drooped over his wide-open mouth. I focus hard, transforming my body into millions of sand granules. Then, I drop them all to the ground, filling in the massive hole in the tracks.

Instantaneously, the wheels of the train press down on me, and I harden my molecules, pushing back up with all of my might. The train is heavy, maybe two tons heavy and at least ten cars long, but I hold my ground, focusing all of my energy on supporting its weight.

Then, after what seems like an eternity, it finally rolls off of me and keeps on chugging.

H-Holy cow! I-I did it?

But there's no time to pat myself on my back, not that I have one right now anyway, because I need to find Grace! I pull my molecules together, forming the shape of a sand spring just like I saw Shaker do, and then propel myself out of the tunnel.

I land with a bounce, relieved to be topside again. It's still night out, but at least there are streetlights. But when I finally come to a stop, I get a surprise.

Someone is pointing a TV news camera at me.

Well, this isn't the best time for an interview. Plus, it won't be long before Shaker's powers wear off and I still need to get myself back together! After all, some of my sandy arm is still with Grace. But where is she?

Then, I feel a pulling sensation to my right.

I follow the feeling, which leads me to a large dumpster. Could it be? I concentrate again, and suddenly, a fountain of sand comes flying out of the dumpster, reattaching to my body!

Whew, I'm whole again! I don't waste any time transforming back to my natural self before my powers wear off. That was certainly a strange experience, but if my sandy arm was inside that dumpster, then that must mean—

"Yuck!" comes a familiar voice.

Suddenly, Grace pops up from inside the dumpster, covered head-to-toe in greenish slime. It takes everything I have not to burst out laughing as a banana peel slides off her forehead.

"One peep and I'll kill you," she says, wiping more banana chunks off her costume. "Now, where's Mover and Shaker? We've got to stop them!"

"Relax," I say. "They got away."

"What?" she says. "How'd that happen?"

"Well, you were unconscious for one," I say. "And then—"

"Um, excuse me," comes a voice from behind.

I turn to find dozens of cameras pointed at us. It's more news people. It's like they all showed up at once.

"Whoa!" Grace says, throwing a leg over the dumpster. "Step back, people. Do I look camera-ready to you? Everyone, please turn off your—"

CRASH!

I look down to find Grace lying on her face.

"Smooth," I say.

"Shut it," she mumbles.

"Excuse me," a female reporter asks, shoving a microphone in my face. "But are you planning to pay for all of this damage?"

"What?" I say. "Um, no. We're with the Freedom Force."

"It doesn't matter if you're an Avenger," she says. "You've probably cost taxpayers millions of dollars in repairs."

"Um, I was just trying to save the day," I answer.

"Do you take responsibility for nearly injuring all of those subway passengers?" a man asks.

"What?" I say. "No. I—I saved them. If it wasn't for me, they could have—"

"Do you believe the Meta population is a menace to society?" another woman asks.

"A... a menace?" I stutter, totally confused.

"I think we're done here," Grace says, finally standing up and blocking the microphones.

"Will you be turning yourselves in for questioning?"

"Excuse me?" I say.

"Grab on," Grace whispers. "We're going back to the Freedom Ferry."

"Do you think you're above the law?"

"Will you be revealing your true identities?"

"Do you think all Metas should be licensed?"

But as the questions keep pouring in, I wrap my arms around Grace, and we take off.

TWO

I GET BLAMED FOR EVERYTHING

Well, I'm feeling less than heroic.

I still don't understand why those reporters were coming after Grace and me like that. I mean, it's not like we were trying to put people in harm's way. We were just doing our jobs—jobs we don't even get paid for!

Plus, Mover and Shaker got away.

So, today has pretty much been an epic fail.

I can tell Grace is miffed as well, because as soon as we got into the Freedom Ferry she barely said two words to me. And when we reached the Waystation, she headed straight for the showers. Not that I blame her. She was buried up to her eyeballs in garbage.

If she wasn't in such a crummy mood, I would have busted her for stinking up the entire shuttle. But I figured she'd had enough humiliation for one day. Besides, as soon as she left I hung four of those pinecone-shaped air fresheners on the rearview mirror.

And just to keep the bad news coming, one of the Freedom Flyers was already parked in the Hangar when we got back, which means some of the team had returned from their mission before we did.

My only hope is that Mom and Dad aren't with them, because if they find out we skipped out to go on a mission of our own, we're going to be in even more trouble. And after today, more trouble is the last thing I need. So, come to think of it, the safest place for me to be right now is probably in my room.

I tiptoe out of the Hangar and head towards my bedroom. Truthfully, Grace isn't the only one that could use a shower—after all, I was hanging on to her smelly body—but my stomach rumbles in objection. It's late and I haven't eaten anything since dinner. No wonder my legs feel shaky. It might be risky, but I need to grab a snack from the Galley.

Using my best stealth moves, I make it there without being seen. But as soon as I step inside my luck runs out.

I hear his scrambling feet before I see him, and then I barely sidestep Dog-Gone like a matador in a bullfight.

"Easy, boy," I whisper, as he slides past me into the hallway. "Quiet!" I plead as he regains his footing. "No, boy. Take it easy. I'm trying not to—oof!"

Suddenly, that mangy mutt is on top of me, pinning me to the floor. I brace myself for the inevitable barrage of slobber, but after the first lick he makes a funny face and starts spitting and sputtering like he's tasted glue.

"Shhh!" I whisper. "Relax, you're not going to die. I've just got Grace's dumpster goo all over me. It's not like you gave me a chance to warn you."

Dog-Gone runs to his water bowl and starts guzzling like he's been wandering through a desert for days. Oh well. I guess now's my best chance to grab some chow and make a quick getaway. I open the fridge when—

"Hey, Elliott."

I jump out of my skin.

Standing behind me is Makeshift!

"Oh, hey," I say casually, leaning against the fridge. I need to stay cool. I can't let him think anything is wrong. "So, you're back, huh? How'd it go?"

"I was going to ask you the same thing," he says, grabbing a bag of tortilla chips from the pantry. "Because the last time I saw you, you were doing your homework—in regular clothes."

I look down. I'm still in my costume. Busted!

"Oh, yeah," I say. "We went out."

"Grace too, huh?" he says. "Anything big?"

"Mover and Shaker," I say. "But they got away. How about you?"

"Strange one," he says. "The Meta Monitor picked

up four unknown Meta 3 signatures at the edge of the Ozone layer. But when we got there, they were gone."

"That is strange," I say. "Well, I guess we both struck out. Um, Mom wasn't with you, was she?"

"Nope," he says, opening the bag of chips.

Yes!

"But your dad was," he says.

Dad? Uh-oh.

"Um, Makeshift," I say, "you wouldn't mind not mentioning anything about—"

"Me?" he says, munching on a chip. "Nah, I never saw ya."

"Thanks," I say. I'm about to bolt when I hear—

"Elliott!"

My back tightens. It's Dad!

"Good luck," Makeshift says.

"Thanks," I say. "I'm gonna need it."

"Elliott!" Dad calls again.

Dog-Gone looks up at me and whimpers.

"See you in the next life, buddy," I say.

"Elliott!"

"Coming!" I yell back.

It sounds like he's in the Lounge. As I make my way over, I run through possible excuses in my head. Maybe I'll blame it on Grace. Yeah, that's it! After all, I just wanted to finish my homework. She's the one who called me a chicken. Or maybe I'll—

"Elliott," Dad says.

Huh? I look up and realize I'm already standing in the Lounge—right in front of Dad!

Oh, boy. What am I going to say?

He's still in costume with one hand on his hip and the other holding the remote control. Then I see Grace sitting on the couch in her pajamas with a pink towel wrapped around her head. She looks really mad.

"Um, am I about to be grounded until I'm a teeny, tiny old man?" I ask.

"Probably," he says. "But right now, take a seat next to your sister and watch this."

Wait, what? My punishment is to watch TV. Really?

"Is he for real?" I ask, sitting next to Grace.

"Yep," she says, staring straight ahead. "It's pretty horrible."

Horrible? Is she crazy? From now on I want Dad to hand out all of my punishments. I slide back on the sofa and throw my feet up on the ottoman. I hope they're watching a movie.

But as I get cozy, I see the TV is tuned to a news station. It's CNC, the popular cable news channel. There are two talking heads on the screen, a blond-haired woman and a very white-haired man with a mustache. I've seen the woman before. Her name is Sarah Anderson, the popular news anchor who hosts the CNC Morning Newsflash. But I've never seen the man before.

He looks kind of intimidating with his piercing blue eyes, military crew cut, and square jaw. Then, titles appear beneath his face with his name.

It reads: *General William Winch.*

"For those viewers just tuning in," Sarah Anderson says, "I'm here with General William Winch, former Chairman of the Joint Chiefs of Staff. So, General, you're serious about this?"

"Dead serious, Ms. Anderson," General Winch says. "Who gave these Metas the right to do whatever they want? It's not in our Constitution, it's not in our Bill of Rights, and I certainly don't know of any laws passed that give Metas special authority to wreak havoc on our society, do you?"

"Well, of course not," Sarah Anderson says. "But not all Metas are bad guys. Take the Freedom Force, for instance. They've saved our planet too many times to count. Surely, you aren't lumping them into that category, are you?"

"Of course I am!" he barks. "Why should they get a free pass to terrorize America?"

"Who does he think he is?" Grace says, slamming her fist into the sofa. "I'd like to see him do what we do!"

"Quiet, dear," Dad says. "Let's see where this goes."

Now I realize why Grace said this is horrible.

This guy is attacking us on television!

"Because they're heroes, General Winch," Sarah Anderson says. "Without them, we probably wouldn't even be sitting here to have this discussion."

"I'm not convinced of that!" General Winch says.

"Your network captured what happened this evening. Run it again and tell me what you see. Because what I see are Meta-humans putting ordinary citizens in danger."

"Yes, sir," Sarah Anderson says, raising an eyebrow. "In fact, we do have that footage and we'll run it one more time for those of you who missed it. This happened tonight in Keystone City's subway system…"

Keystone City's subway system?

Oh, jeez. I drop my head in my hands.

The footage starts, accompanied by the voice of a male reporter. "Today, on the 'L' line in Keystone City's subway system, two Meta children playing superhero attempted to stop a pair of Meta villains from making off with millions of dollars in stolen gemstones. Not surprisingly, the villains got away, but not before the foursome caused an incredible amount of damage to the infrastructure and nearly derailed a subway train filled with innocent passengers."

"Hang on!" I say. "That's not what happened!"

Suddenly, the screen cuts to a grainy, black-and-white image of Grace and I running through a subway tunnel. Then, it switches to Shaker in the shape of a giant hammer smashing the tracks. And then it cuts to Mover busting a hole in the tunnel ceiling. Suddenly, a piece of debris flies towards the camera, and the screen goes black.

"Hey!" I blurt out. "The camera got smashed before it showed me saving all of those people!"

Just then, the image switches to a closeup of Grace inside the dumpster with the banana peel on her head.

"OMG!" she shrieks, shriveling into a ball. "This is so embarrassing!"

I'm about to laugh, but the next thing I know my face is plastered on the screen. Microphones are pointed at me and reporters are peppering me with questions. I look totally clueless, like a deer in headlights. Then, it cuts to Grace and I flying away.

"Well, that didn't look good," I mutter.

"Quiet," Dad says firmly.

Sarah Anderson and General Winch are back.

"The evidence is right there," General Winch says. "You know what Meta heroes do? They escalate situations. If those inexperienced children hadn't interfered, those crooks would have gone away peacefully. But instead, they put hundreds of lives in danger while costing taxpayers millions of dollars in repairs. We have laws restricting ordinary citizens from carrying weapons in public. Shouldn't we have laws restricting Metas from using deadly superpowers in public?"

"I hear you," Sarah Anderson says. "But I'm not sure most citizens would agree with you."

"Public opinion is changing, Ms. Anderson," General Winch says, staring right at the camera. "And I won't rest until something is done about it."

Suddenly, Dad turns off the television.

Well, that was disturbing.

"I'm ruined," Grace mutters, slumping into the couch. "That'll never come off of social media."

"Grace, that's not important," Dad says.

"Of course it's important, Dad!" Grace says. "I'll be a GIF forever!"

"Okay, okay," he says. "I get it. But you heard that General. He's on a crusade against Meta heroes."

"But why?" I ask.

"I don't know," Dad says. "But what I do know is that neither of you asked for permission before jetting off to save the day. I think now would be a good time to discuss proper punishment."

"Punishment?" Grace says. "Don't you think I've suffered enough? Believe me, I'm sorry. This horror show will haunt me for the rest of my life."

"And what about you, Elliott?" Dad asks.

"Well, honestly, I'm totally confused," I say, crossing my arms. "I mean, I get it that we took off against your wishes, but we were only doing what heroes are supposed to do. Should we really be punished for that? Yeah, I get there was some damage and stuff. But doesn't that just come with the territory?"

"Elliott…" Dad starts.

But suddenly, the phone rings.

That's weird. Ever since we got rid of the Prop House, the phone never rings. Who could it be? I mean, we live in freaking outer space!

Dad picks it up.

"Hello?" he says into the receiver. "Yes, this is Freedom Force headquarters. Yes, we are in space. Yes, that is pretty cool. This is Captain Justice. With whom am I speaking?"

Grace and I look at each other.

"CNC news?" he says, raising his eyebrows. "The two kids on the footage? Yes, they are members of the Freedom Force. Yes, the girl with the banana on her head is Glory Girl."

"See!" Grace exclaims, burying her face in a pillow.

"The boy?" Dad says, looking at me. "Yes, he's here. Yes, I'm sure he's a member of the Freedom Force. His name is Epic Zero. Epic... Z-E-R-O. Yes, he really is a hero. You'd like to speak to him?"

Wait, what?

"Epic Zero," Dad says, "it's for you."

"Him?" Grace says, lifting her face. "Why him?"

"Um, hello?" I say, taking the phone.

"Is this Mr. Zero?" a female voice asks.

"Yes," I say.

"Great," she says. "Listen, I'm the Production Assistant for the CNC Morning Newsflash, and Ms. Anderson would love to interview you on tomorrow morning's broadcast. What do you say?"

"Um, what?" I say.

"I know this may come as a shock," she continues, "but you're trending as the hottest topic in the country right now. Of course, some people are defending what you did, but others are questioning your motives and the motives of all superheroes. This is your opportunity for people to hear directly from you. This is your chance to represent all caped crusaders."

"What do they want?" Grace asks, waving her hand impatiently in my face.

"They want to interview me," I say, covering the receiver. "They want me to talk about what happened."

"What?" Grace says, throwing her pillow to the ground. "Why does he get all of the luck?"

"Mr. Zero, are you still there?"

"Um, yes, I'm still here," I say.

"So, are you interested in appearing?" she asks. "Or do you want people to be against superheroes?"

"Against?" I say. "Well, no, I don't want that."

"So, you will appear?" she asks, more as a statement than a question.

"Well... I... I guess I have to," I say.

"Great!" she says. "We'll start promoting it now. And don't worry, millions of people will be tuned in to your every word. Get a good night's sleep because we'll see you bright and early at CNC Headquarters. We tape live at seven o'clock. Goodbye."

Uh, did she just say, 'millions of people?' And 'live?'

You know, maybe this isn't such a good idea.

I'm about to pull out when I suddenly hear a CLICK followed by a dial tone. The phone is dead.

And apparently, so am I.

Meta Profile

Mover and Shaker

⬜ Name: Mover	⬜ Name: Shaker
⬜ Status: Villain/Active	⬜ Status: Villain/Active
⬜ META 2: Meta-morph	⬜ META 2: Meta-morph
⬜ Body made of rock	⬜ Body made of sand
⬜ Considerable Strength	⬜ Considerable Shapeshifting
⬜ Considerable Invulnerability	⬜ Particles return to core body

THREE

I MAKE A FOOL OF MYSELF

In about ten minutes I'm going to look like a total goober on live television.

What a nightmare.

I mean, it's way too early in the morning, and I'm stuck in the green room at CNC headquarters, pacing back and forth like I'm about to be sent to the principal's office. There are millions of thoughts running through my brain, but none of them are clear because I didn't sleep a wink. Instead, I spent the entire night tossing and turning, freaked out of my mind.

Believe me, I'm kicking myself for not backing out of this in time. Of course, Dad tried to reassure me by telling me everything would be fine. According to him, it's moments like this that build character. I told him I don't need more stinking character!

At least Mom was on my side. When she got back to the Waystation and found out what happened, she was clearly concerned. And based on the number of strange facial expressions Mom and Dad were making at one another, it looked like they were having some pretty intense telepathic arguments. Unfortunately, despite how Mom may have felt about the situation, she told me I had to follow through on my commitment.

So, I tried the next best thing—pawning it off on Grace. After all, she's the one who wants to be the big-time celebrity—not me.

But she wasn't having it.

Even though she was clearly jealous when I first got the call, she claimed her reputation was shattered and she needed to lay low for a while. She called it something like 'image crisis management.' She said she wasn't going to do any public appearances until her fans forgot about her banana-on-the-head footage.

Good luck with that!

So here I am.

Just. Freaking. Wonderful.

Honestly, being on camera isn't my thing. Just knowing millions of people are watching my every move makes me want to hurl. To say I'm not looking forward to this is a gross understatement.

Suddenly, there's a KNOCK and the door opens.

"One minute, Mr. Zero," says a woman wearing a headset. Then, she shuts the door.

Awesome. I can't wait.

"Relax," Dad says. "You'll do fine."

"You sure about that?" Grace says. "Because he looks like he's gonna puke."

"Then why don't you do it?" I offer.

"No dice," she says, buffing her nails. "I'm on a temporary hiatus. Besides, they wanted you."

"You've got this," Dad says. "Just remember what we talked about. Be honest about how you feel and everything will be fine. Remember, you're representing all Meta heroes out there."

"Gee, that'll help me relax," I mutter.

I sure wish Mom was here, but she thought it would be best if she stayed behind. When she kissed me goodbye, she looked more nervous for me than I was. So that's probably not a good thing.

"Hey," Grace says, "your mask is crooked."

As I adjust it, the door pops open.

"It's time," the woman says.

"Well, it's been a great life," I say. "Say goodbye to Dog-Gone for me."

"Don't be silly," Dad says, patting my back. "You've got this."

"Break a leg," Grace says.

"I wish," I say, following the woman into the hall.

As we walk, I try not to hyperventilate. The woman

starts talking to me, but I'm so busy thinking about what I'm going to say I only catch a few words, like:

"Two segments—Debate—Questions—Okay?"

"Um, what?" I say.

"Are you okay?" she asks.

"Yeah," I say, lying through my teeth. "I'm fine."

"Great," she says, pushing me forward. "Because it's showtime. And whatever you do, don't drink from Ms. Anderson's mug. She hates that."

Suddenly, I realize we're on set!

It's a real TV studio, with bright lights, big cameras, and tons of people milling about. A man with a clipboard appears and attaches a microphone to the front of my costume. Then, he grabs my arm, and pulls me onto the stage, placing me in the center of three chairs behind a desk. I look over my shoulder at the big monitors filled with floating CNC logos.

"Eyes this way, kid," the man says, now standing in front. Then, he holds up his fingers and starts counting down. "And five, four—"

Suddenly, a blond-haired woman in a dark business suit plops into the seat on my right. She looks strangely familiar. Then, I realize it's Sarah Anderson herself!

OMG! This is about to happen!

"You look much smaller in person," she whispers.

"—one!" the man says.

I stare straight at the center camera and realize millions of people are watching me right now. I'm gonna hurl.

"Welcome to the CNC Morning Newsflash," Sarah Anderson says. "I'm Sarah Anderson, and as promised, our lead story this morning is the highly controversial topic being debated nationwide. Meta heroes—good guys or dangers to society? We're fortunate to have with us one of the Meta heroes responsible for the massive destruction that occurred yesterday in Keystone City's subway system. Surprisingly, he is an actual member of the Freedom Force who goes by the name of Epic Zebra. Welcome to the hot seat, Mr. Zebra."

"Um, thanks," I say. "But my name is Epic Z—"

"Mr. Zebra," she interrupts, "several prominent citizens are calling Meta heroes a menace to society. In your opinion, is that true?"

"W What?" I say. "Oh no. We're heroes."

"Interesting," Sarah Anderson says. "But how can you call yourself heroes when your actions result in so much collateral damage?"

"Well," I say, "we don't mean to cause damage. We're trying to stop the bad guys who will do anything to get what they want. Without us, who would stop them?"

"Good point," Sarah Anderson says.

Gee, this isn't so bad. Maybe it'll be okay after all.

Suddenly, a figure sits down to my left.

I turn and do a double take.

It's a man with a crewcut wearing a dark suit.

I feel like I've seen him before. Then, it hits me!

It's General Winch!

What's he doing here?

"I see the other member of our panel has finally arrived," Sarah Anderson says. "Welcome, General Winch. You are the most outspoken critic of Meta heroes like Mr. Zebra here. What do you say to his response?"

"My apologies for being late," he says politely. "I was just speaking with the President." Then, he looks at me and his face turns bright red. "This child is asking who would stop those Meta criminals if superheroes weren't around? That's easy. Law enforcement professionals, that's who! The police. The Air Force. The Army. Highly trained professionals who follow proper safety procedures, unlike these costumed vigilantes who constantly put the public at risk."

Wow! He's so angry he's spitting everywhere.

"Your response, Mr. Zebra," Sarah Anderson asks.

"I—I—um…", I stammer. My mind is racing. I don't know what to say. I wasn't prepared to argue with this guy!

"Perhaps we should roll the footage again," Sarah Anderson says quickly. "That should help you out."

Suddenly, the video of yesterday's subway debacle starts playing on the monitors behind us.

"You okay, kid?" Sarah Anderson whispers. "You're slowing down the show here. This is a debate program. That means you actually have to debate him."

"Um, sorry," I say.

My throat feels really dry. I need some water or something. Then, I notice a mug in front of me. I grab it and take a sip, but as soon as the liquid goes into my mouth, I spit it back out.

"Yuck! What's that?"

"My coffee," Sarah Anderson says, clearly annoyed.

Then, the video ends on a frame of Grace with the banana peel on her head.

"And we're back," Sarah Anderson says. "Mr. Zebra, after viewing yesterday's battle in the subway station, how do you respond to General Winch's accusations that all Meta heroes are untrained vigilantes?"

I open my mouth but nothing comes out. Suddenly, my skin feels super warm. Boy, those stage lights are hot. I wipe beads of sweat from my forehead. Then, I notice the clipboard guy waving at me, encouraging me to say something. But I feel like I'm going to pass out.

"How about some statistics then?" Sarah Anderson jumps in. "According to the accountants, your actions will cost Keystone City over thirteen million dollars in repairs. And the 'L' line is scheduled to be out of service for up to six months. What do you have to say about that?"

Wow, that's a lot of time and money.

"Not to mention innocent lives were nearly lost," General Winch adds. "There's no price tag for that."

"Mr. Zebra?"

"I... um," I mutter. "C-Can I use the bathroom?"

"Okaaay," Sarah Anderson says. "This sounds like a

great time for a commercial break. We'll be right back with this stimulating debate about Meta heroes."

"And cut," the guy with the clipboard announces.

"Listen, kid," Sarah Anderson says. "You've got to pull it together. He's eating you alive out there. If you're going to defend superheroes, you've only got one more segment to do it."

"Okay," I say, standing up.

But as I move past the General, he smirks and says, "Are you really the best they've got?"

I brush past him and head off-stage. The woman with the headset meets me and points me to a nearby room. It's the bathroom!

"Um, you should probably give me your microphone before you go in there," she says.

"Oh yeah," I say, popping it off and handing it over.

Then, I push open the door and lock it behind me.

Thank goodness I'm alone! Truthfully, I didn't have to go to the bathroom, but I needed to get out of there. I mean, what am I doing? I can only imagine what Dad and Grace are thinking. I'm making a total fool of myself!

Why am I letting that guy get under my skin? What does he know about facing Meta villains? I'd like to see him take down Mover and Shaker.

But why can't I tell him that?

I lean over the sink and look into the mirror.

Yep, I look exactly like I feel. My skin is red, my eyes are puffy, and my hair is an absolute mess.

I splash cold water on my face to cool down. I need to speak up. I need to—

"Elliott Harkness."

Huh?

My head nearly hits the faucet, because when I look into the mirror, I'm not alone!

Standing behind me are four men.

But by their faces, they aren't men at all!

In fact, they're not even human!

One has a face like a bug, another looks like a horse, and the other two... well, they don't look like anything I've ever seen before. Then, I notice they're all wearing blue uniforms with yellow stripes on their shoulders.

Wait, I know those uniforms!

"Y-You're Intergalactic Paladins!" I say.

They don't answer but I know I'm right. Their uniforms are just like the one Proog was wearing when I met him at ArmaTech—in the past! Poor Proog. He never stood a chance against that slimeball Norman Fairchild. Man, that was one of the hardest missions I've ever had.

Then, I realize they're all holding silver wands—Infinity Wands—and I shudder. The last time I saw an Infinity Wand, I accidentally destroyed it, giving birth to Meta-Taker!

"Meta readings are confirmed," horse-face says, waving his wand over my head. "He's an exact match."

An exact match? To what?

"Listen, fellas," I say, "I'd love to help you out, but now's not a good time. See, I've got to get out of this bathroom here and go finish a TV show. You do realize we're all standing in a bathroom, right?"

"Elliott Harkness, you are being placed under arrest for aiding in the escape of a notorious intergalactic felon," bug-head says. "You will stand before the Interstellar Court of Law to defend your crimes."

"The Interstellar what?" I say. "What crimes?"

Suddenly, it occurs to me I should probably get out of here. And fast.

"Now," horse-face says.

But before I can move, the four Paladins raise their wands and there's a blinding flash of light.

And we're gone.

Meta Profile

General Winch

Name: William Winch	Height: 6'1"
Race: Human	Weight: 213 lbs
Status: Hero/Active	Eyes/Hair: Blue/White

META 0: No Powers	Observed Characteristics	
	Combat 20	
Former Chairman of the Joint Chiefs of Staff	Durability 15	Leadership 98
Former 5-Star General	Strategy 95	Willpower 90

FOUR

I FACE JAIL TIME

When I open my eyes, we're no longer in the bathroom.

In fact, I don't think we're even on Earth!

That's because other than the four Intergalactic Paladins surrounding me, there's nothing else I recognize.

We're standing inside a massive stadium that's open to a purple sky with two moons! Beneath my feet is a red track encircling a fifty-foot wide gray disc sitting smack dab in the center. And to add to the weirdness, there's a big black cube floating twenty feet above the disc.

Yep, we're definitely not on Earth anymore.

I'm about to ask my captors where they've taken me when I realize we're not alone. The stadium's stands are filled with people. Except they aren't people at all.

They're more aliens!

Aliens wearing Paladin uniforms!

Then it hits me. I know exactly where I am.

I'm on the home planet of the Intergalactic Paladins!

"Turn and face the Council," horse-face demands.

Council? What Council? It's not until I spin around that I see seven more aliens sitting on a platform behind me. Huh? Where'd they come from?

But unlike the Intergalactic Paladins, these guys are all wearing robes—black robes—like judges.

I don't know what's going on, but by the glum expressions on their faces, I'd say we're not off to a good start. Then, the green, scaly guy in the middle pulls himself up with his large staff and shuffles to the edge of the platform, his fishy eyes fixed on me.

I take a deep breath. Okay, I'm sure this is just a big misunderstanding. I'll be back home in no time.

"Elliott Harkness of Earth," he bellows, "welcome to Paladin Planet. I am Quovaar, Supreme Justice of the Interstellar Council, and you are accused of committing unspeakable crimes against the universe!"

Then again, maybe not.

"The charges against you are serious," he continues, "and you will stand trial for your actions."

"Stand trial?" I blurt out. "For what?"

"Heed my warning, Elliott Harkness," Quovaar says, "ignorance will not serve you well here. But to ensure there are no flaws in our proceedings, I shall formally state the charges against you. First, you stand accused of unlawfully destroying an Infinity Wand. Second, you are charged with aiding and abetting the escape of Krule the Conqueror from the 13th Dimension. The prosecution will demonstrate that you committed these crimes willingly and with malicious intent, endangering the lives of billions who wish to live in peace."

Wait, what?

Did he just say Krule escaped from the 13th Dimension? And for some reason, they think I helped him? That's nuts!

"Um, pardon me," I say. "But you've got this all wrong. That's not exactly what—"

"Tell us, Elliott Harkness," Quovaar interjects, pointing his staff towards the center of the arena. "Does this look familiar?"

My eyes follow his sweeping arm to the hovering black cube. Suddenly, it splits in half, exposing a purple object. My jaw drops.

"The Cosmic Key!" I exclaim as a chill runs down my spine. Supposedly, the Cosmic Key is the only key that can open the 13th Dimension.

"Yes," Quovaar says. "Your positive identification of the Cosmic Key is noted for the record. But by your reaction, I assume you are surprised to see it in our possession? After all, it has taken decades for us to recover it. But recover it we have, although too late to prevent Krule's escape."

My mind is racing. I mean, the last time I saw the Cosmic Key was like, thirty years ago when I used TechnocRat's Time Warper device to go back into the past to fix my present. In fact, I was about to destroy the Cosmic Key and rid the world of Meta-Taker forever, but at the last second one of the Time Trotter's Pterodactyls appeared out of nowhere and snatched it away. Then, Krule's ugly, three-eyed mug appeared and he bragged about how he'd take over the universe.

Now that he's free, is that what he's doing?

And why do they think I helped him? How are they even coming to that conclusion?

"Listen," I start. "I—"

"I recommend saving your arguments for your defense," Quovaar says. "Your trial will commence tomorrow upon the rising of the three suns. Per the Order of the Paladin, you will be permitted to call upon one witness to support your testimony, and the final verdict of guilty or not guilty will be revealed by the power of the Paladin's Pulse."

The power of the Paladin's what?

Suddenly, Quovaar raises his arms, and a giant, pulsating egg rises from behind the platform. The thing is huge, nearly the size of a hot-air balloon. But as I look closer, I realize that the big egg is made up of hundreds of smaller eggs, each white in color.

What is that thing?

"This is the Paladin's Pulse," Quovaar continues,

"the most unbiased legal system in the universe. Each individual sphere on the surface of the Paladin's Pulse is perfectly attuned to the inner conscience of one Paladin present. If the majority of spheres turn red at the conclusion of your trial, you will be found guilty. However, if the majority of spheres are green, you will be declared innocent."

"Hang on a sec," I say, cleaning out my ears. "Do you mean this huge egg thing is gonna reveal if everyone thinks I'm innocent?"

"Or guilty," Quovaar says, narrowing his eyes.

Now I'm totally confused. I mean, the way Proog talked about the Intergalactic Paladins made them seem like noble, peace-loving heroes. Yet, I'm getting the feeling these guys are thirsty for blood. It's like they're ready to send me down the river no matter what the truth may be.

"Look," I say, "I'm not sure what's going on here, but I'm a hero just trying to save lives, and occasionally the universe. I'm not sure you've got the right guy."

"Maric?" Quovaar says. "Your reading?"

Suddenly, horse-face steps forward.

"Yes, Supreme Justice," Maric says with a low bow. "This child's Meta signature corresponds precisely with the Meta signature from Proog's Infinity Wand."

Proog's Wand? What's he talking about?

But then it all comes back to me. When I was trying to stop Norman Fairchild, I absorbed a tremendous amount of Meta energy from the unconscious Skelton known as the Blood Master. And that Meta energy came directly from Proog's Infinity Wand!

Holy cow!

It must have stuck to me!

"Then it is confirmed," Quovaar says. "Elliott Harkness, tonight you will have ample time to build your case while in our prison. Be forewarned that here on Paladin Planet it is useless to use your Meta powers. You are surrounded by hundreds of Intergalactic Paladins, all of whom have been granted the authority to take whatever actions are necessary to subdue you if you try to escape—including your death."

I swallow hard. As I look into the stands, I see hundreds of bright lights. All of the Paladins have activated their Infinity Wands in a show of force!

"Consider wisely who you will call upon as a witness," Quovaar continues. "That individual will provide the only testimony used for your defense. Tomorrow, upon the rising of the three suns, your trial will begin. If you are found innocent, you will be cleared of all charges and returned to your home. But if you are found guilty, you will be punished."

"P-Punished?" I say. "What does that mean?"

"Per the Order of the Paladin," Quovaar says, "if you are found guilty you will be banished to the 13th Dimension."

Suddenly, the disc in the center slides open and I'm

staring into a circle of swirling, purple energy.

No. Freaking. Way.

That must be the 13th Dimension!

"Try to get some rest," Quovaar says. "Because what happens tomorrow will determine your fate forever."

***

Well, I certainly didn't see this coming.

Somehow, I went from flunking a debate on live television to sitting inside an alien prison being charged with crimes I didn't commit. I couldn't have predicted this one with a crystal ball.

I wonder what Dad and Grace are thinking. I'm sure they think I ran away from the CNC building and went into hiding. Not that I blame them. I know I made a fool of myself up there. Unfortunately, that'll be the last memory they'll have of me because I'll probably never see them again.

I take in my bleak surroundings. It's me, a concrete floor, and a whole lot of prison bars. And to add to the ambiance, the whole place smells like gym socks.

Lovely.

I sit down on the floor and stretch out my sore arms. Boy, those Paladins who carried me down three flights of stairs were rough. Of course, I'm sure all of the other prisoners they carted me past are even rougher. I hope I'm in solitary confinement because I don't want to run into any of them.

I mean, I'm no criminal. At least I don't think I am.

Technically, I did destroy Proog's Infinity Wand, but I was only acting in self-defense. If I didn't blow it up, Fairchild would have used it to obliterate me. Of course, I also ended up creating Meta-Taker in the process.

So, who knows? Maybe I should be sent to the 13th Dimension for that alone.

I think back to my conversation with Proog. He said the 13th Dimension is where the Intergalactic Paladins put the most dangerous criminals in the galaxy. And once you're sent there you not only lose your powers, but you also live forever.

Wonderful.

I get to spend eternity with Meta villains who will never die.

That is, unless I can prove my innocence.

Quovaar said I can call upon one witness, so I run through my options. Of course, Mom and Dad come to mind first, but since they're my parents I'm not sure they'd be considered objective. Grace? Nah, she might actually want me banished to the 13th Dimension. There's Dog-Gone, but all he has to offer is slobber.

I go through the rest of the Freedom Force.

TechnocRat is so annoying they'd probably throw the book at me. Makeshift started as a villain, so that won't work. Blue Bolt talks too fast. Master Mime can't talk at all. Shadow Hawk is a possibility, but he'd probably lecture everyone on right versus wrong which wouldn't work in my favor.

So, my options are pretty limited.

I wonder how I'll look in an orange jumpsuit.

"Pssst," comes a sharp whisper.

I look through the bars and see some alien dude staring at me from the cell across the hall. He's bald, with white skin, and big red eyes. He's sitting on the floor cross-legged and wearing a red uniform.

"Pssst," he repeats, this time standing up and wrapping his fingers around his cell door. "Are you deaf, kid?"

"No," I say. "What do you want?"

"To pass the time," he says. "My name is Caliban. What's yours?"

At first, I'm reluctant to tell him. But then I remember I'm in prison, so what do I have to lose?

"I'm Epic Zero."

"Epic Zero, huh?" he says. "You're a little young for this place, aren't you? Must be a good story as to why you're here."

"It's a long story," I say. "Honestly, I'm still trying to figure it out myself."

"Ha," he says. "Well, we've got plenty of time for stories around here—long or otherwise. How about if I tell you mine first?"

"Sure," I say. "Why not?"

"Okay, then," Caliban says, leaning against his cell

door. "You see, I'm no crook. I was the captain of a cargo ship. We prided ourselves on making deliveries on time. If it absolutely, positively had to be there by the next lunar cycle, you'd call us. Life was good until we took a job in the Trans-Neptunian region. Everything was going smoothly until we picked up a bunch of strange readings on our radar. At first, we thought it was a taxi fleet, but then we realized we were being chased by warships."

Warships?

Like, Skelton warships?

"We tried outrunning them," he continues, "but we had no chance. They were first-class vehicles, top of the line. Of course, we sent out a distress signal, but as they closed in, we knew we were doomed because on their hull was a symbol—a three-eyed skull and crossbones."

"Three eyes?" I ask.

"Exactly," Caliban says. "These weren't just any warships. These were pirate ships, manned by Krule the Conqueror and his Motley Crew."

Krule? So there's my proof. He did escape!

"Honestly, I thought I was seeing a ghost," Caliban says. "Last I heard, Krule and his men were trapped in the 13th Dimension, yet it was clearly him. He overtook us in no time, but instead of shooting us down, he boarded us. I'll never forget that strange third eye. As soon as it lit up, my crew walked onto his ship like they were robots!"

Yep, that's him all right.

"Yet, for some reason, he didn't hypnotize me," Caliban says. "Krule said my men were his now. Then, he had them load a giant black box into my cargo hold and told me to head straight for Paladin Planet. He said 'they' would always be on his tail as long as he had this box in his possession. I asked him who 'they' were and what was in the box, but he said it was none of my business. He warned that if I didn't do as he said, my men's lives would be at risk. After that, he took off with his fleet."

Hang on. Did he say a 'giant black box?'

Does that mean—?

"I knew he was a man of his word, and if I disobeyed, he would punish my men. I couldn't live with myself if something happened to my lads, so I followed his instructions. But as soon as I entered Paladin Planet's atmosphere, I was intercepted by a squadron of Paladins who took over my ship. When they opened the black box. I'll never forget what was inside. It was this strange purple key. They called it the—"

"—Cosmic Key!" I blurt out.

"The very one," he says. "They accused me of helping Krule hide evidence of his escape and dumped me in here. My trial was set for tomorrow but for some reason, it's been delayed. But I don't plan on sticking around."

Then, he looks suspiciously from side-to-side and whispers, "Because we're busting out of here. Tonight."

"Um, excuse me?" I whisper back. "Did you just say

you're busting out of here… tonight?"

"Yeah, tonight," he says. "Do you think anyone around here really has a shot at a fair trial? I'm not going into the 13th Dimension. We're breaking out at midnight. Do you want to come along?"

"Wow," I say. I mean, I wasn't expecting that. Then again, I wasn't expecting to be here at all. But Caliban's words echo in my brain. *Do you think anyone around here really has a shot at a fair trial?'*

What if he's right? I mean, I know I'm innocent but what if the trial is rigged? What if they're planning on setting me up? I could end up banished to the 13th Dimension no matter what I say!

But something is holding me back.

"Um, I'll think about it," I say. "But how are you gonna do it? I mean, Paladins are crawling all over the place."

"Oh, don't worry about that," Caliban says, nodding towards the cell to his left. "We've got him."

Him? Who's him?

But as I stoop down to get a better look into Caliban's neighboring cell, I see a hulking figure sitting on the floor—a figure with long, curved horns on his head.

OMG!

I-I know him!

It's… Aries?

Meta Profile

Quovaar

Name: Quovaar	Height: 6'0"
Race: Unknown	Weight: 190 lbs
Status: Hero/Active	Eyes/Hair: Green/Bald

META 3: Magic	Observed Characteristics	
Supreme Justice of the Inter-stellar Court of Law	Combat 98	
	Durability 51	Leadership 100
Member of the Intergalactic Paladins	Strategy 100	Willpower 100

FIVE

I BUST A MOVE

Midnight comes way faster than I expected.

Ever since I learned about Caliban's crazy plan I've been pacing back and forth in my cell like a caged animal. I mean, is he serious? How's he going to bust out of here? This place is swarming with Paladins!

Just thinking about it freaks me out.

But Caliban doesn't look worried in the least.

According to him, his plan is foolproof. He said he's been watching the guards closely for days now, and there's a one-minute window where they leave the prison to switch shifts—right at the stroke of midnight. That's when he's planning to make his move.

That sounds great in theory, but honestly, I'm not so sure that's the best idea. But then again, what other options do I have? Based on Quovaar's tone, my trial is probably just a formality. If I were a betting man, I'd say I'm destined for a date with the 13th Dimension!

And that's the last place I want to be!

The only part of Caliban's plan giving me any shred of hope is having Aries on our side. After all, Aries and I fought together on Arena World, and I know he's as tough as they come. Plus, we're both members of the Zodiac which is a pretty unique bond.

So, you'd think I'd be feeling more optimistic, but there's one teeny-tiny thing making me uneasy.

Aries won't talk to me.

I don't know why, but every time I try getting his attention he doesn't respond. Instead, he just sits there like a brooding rock. I've got no clue what's wrong.

After all, the Aries I remember had major swagger. When I asked Caliban about it, he said Aries has been like this ever since he arrived, but not to worry because Aries is aligned with the plan. That's great news, but it also raises a question:

What is Aries even doing here?

I mean, he's a big-time Meta hero. I'm here because of a big misunderstanding. But why is Aries on Paladin Planet? I couldn't imagine him committing a crime.

But I guess I'll have to wait for that answer, because just then Caliban walks up to his cell door, looks up and down the hall, and declares: "Now!"

Now?

Wait. Does he mean, like, 'now, now?'

RIP! CLANG!

There's an ear-splitting noise to my right, and when I turn Aries is tossing the front door of his cell to the ground! Seconds later, he's in the corridor, and with two more ear-jarring yanks, he's ripped off the doors to Caliban's cell, and mine too!

Suddenly, SIRENS wail.

"Let's go!" Caliban says.

They take off, but for a split second, I'm frozen. I mean, am I really going to do this? As soon as I step out of this cell, I'll look totally guilty.

"Come on!" Caliban yells. "It's your only chance!"

Caliban falls in behind Aries who is bulldozing his way down the hall. But my mind is still spinning. If I go with them, I'm basically telling the Interstellar Council I'm guilty. But if I stay and lose the trial, I'll be doomed forever!

I-I don't know what to do.

I lean forward. Caliban and Aries are nearly gone. Suddenly, my heart starts racing. I can't stay here. I mean, I shouldn't even be here. This may be my only chance.

"Wait for me!" I call, catching up to them.

I brush past the outstretched arms of other prisoners, but I ignore their pleas. There's no way I'm stopping to free them. I mean, who knows what they did to get put in here?

"What do we do now?" I ask.

"Now we get my ship," Caliban says. "Then, I can fly us off of this planet. We just have to break into the impound yard where they keep the confiscated vehicles."

"Great," I say, "where's that?"

"Next to the stadium," he says.

"Oh," I say. "You mean the stadium where all of the Intergalactic Paladins hang out? Great plan."

Seconds later we're in the stairwell.

I figure this little jailbreak will go one of two ways. Either we're clobbered and somehow manage to escape, or we're clobbered and thrown back in jail. Either way, a clobbering is coming.

Why does this stuff always happen to me?

"Hey!" comes a shout from down the hall.

I look up to find three Paladins heading our way! I stop dead in my tracks, ready to retreat, but the next thing I know, Aries rears back his giant fist and pummels them with one punch, sending them flying like bowling pins!

Let the clobbering begin!

"Move!" Caliban yells.

Aries leaps the entire staircase in one bound, while Caliban takes the steps three at a time. I'm huffing and puffing behind, stair by measly stair.

Man, I really need to do more cardio!

I hear more commotion, and by the time I reach the top level, I step over six more unconscious Paladins. I'm impressed. I remember Aries being tough, but I don't remember him being this tough! As I step outside, I find

Aries and Caliban getting their bearings.

Caliban is pointing left and I see the stadium in the distance. Then, I see a bunch of ships parked behind a tall gate next door. That must be the impound yard!

More SIRENS blare.

But this one sounds different. Caliban stops to listen.

"That signal means 'all-hands on deck,'" Caliban says, "They're calling the entire force into action. Let's go!"

But we're too late.

Because when I look up into the sky, dozens of bright lights are heading our way.

If I have any chance of surviving this pummeling, I can't rely on my own physical prowess. So, I concentrate hard, pulling in Aries' powers of Super-strength, and then I'm ready to go.

"Stick with me," I tell Caliban, grabbing his wrist.

"Wait," he says, "what are you—"

But before he can finish, I tuck him under my arm like a football and jump, hurtling a ridiculous distance. I stay close behind Aries, who is clearing a path in front of us, knocking Paladin after Paladin out of the air.

Seconds later, the impound yard is within range. There must be hundreds of ships in there. I can't believe it, we're actually going to make it!

BOOM!

Then, Aries gets creamed.

I shield my eyes as we fly through the debris, but

Aries isn't so lucky. He drops to the ground like a bomb, sending up tons of rubble. As soon as I touch down, I put on the brakes, kicking up a huge dust cloud.

"Don't stop!" Caliban demands. "Keep going!"

"But Aries is back there," I say. "We can't just leave him."

"Do it!" Caliban yells. "Or we're dead!"

I look up and I know he's right. The Paladins are gaining in number, circling above us like vultures. But I can't just leave Aries. He's my friend.

"I just need a second," I say, putting Caliban on his feet before running towards Aries.

"Fool!" Caliban says, bolting towards the impound yard, drawing half of the Paladins with him.

But I can't stop to help him, I need to get to Aries.

I stumble down the newly formed crater with Aries lying at its center.

"Are you okay?" I ask.

"Better than him," Aries grunts, sitting up.

"Nooooo!" comes a scream.

Looking up, I see a squad of Paladins blasting Caliban into submission.

"Caliban!" I yell.

"No," Aries says, standing up. "He's not Caliban. His real name is Xenox Xanth. He's one of Krule's key lieutenants."

"Wait, what?" I say. "You mean, he lied to us?"

"No," Aries says. "He lied to you. I knew who he

was the second I laid eyes on him. Now stay alert. Here comes trouble."

I look up to see the rest of the Paladins heading our way! I'm about to grab more of Aries' power, when—

THOOM!

Suddenly, the Paladins are blown miles away!

I turn to find Aries with his arms outstretched and palms together.

"Thunderclap," he says. "Let's get to the stadium."

"The stadium?" I say. "But what about the impound yard?"

"That was Xenox's plan," he says. "My plan was always the stadium. I only told him I was following his plan because I figured he might be a useful distraction. Looks like I was right."

I look over to find Caliban, or rather Xenox, being arrested. But I'm totally confused. Why is Aries going to the stadium? But before I can ask him, he says—

"Follow me," and he's off.

Well, unless I want to be captured by the Paladins, I have no choice, but my mind is totally mixed up right now. I have no clue what's going on. And that's not a great feeling.

Aries leaps over the stadium wall and I'm right behind him, landing on the dirt infield. This time, there aren't any Paladins around, but I'm sure that won't last long. My eyes immediately go to the black box floating over the gray disc. Is what Caliban—or Xenox—or whatever his name is—told me about the black box also a lie? Did Krule really ambush his ship, or did Krule intentionally send Xenox to Paladin Planet with the Cosmic Key on board?

I shudder. Just being near the Cosmic Key makes me nervous. Then, I get a bad thought. Is Aries after the Cosmic Key? Is that what he wants?

I don't know, but I do know one thing, I'm sick and tired of not getting the full story. I mean, why didn't Aries tell me Xenox was a phony?

And what else hasn't he told me?

"Okay," I say. "Spill it. What are we doing here?"

"I'm on a rescue mission," Aries says.

"A rescue mission?" I say. "Um, sorry if you haven't noticed, but aren't we the ones who need rescuing around here?"

"No," he says. "I'm here to save Wind Walker."

My eyebrows hit my hairline.

Wind Walker?

The last time I saw Wind Walker was when he saved me from the Rising Suns and worm-holed me into Elliott 2's universe. After that, he said he was going to try to solve the riddle of the Blur, but I never heard from him again. In fact, I even tried calling for him in the Hydrostation but he never appeared. I always wondered what happened to him.

"Are you saying Wind Walker is here?" I ask. "On Paladin Planet?"

"No," Aries says, pointing down. "He's not here. He's in there."

But as I follow his finger my jaw drops, because he's pointing right at the gray disc.

But—But that's the cover to the... the...

"Wind Walker is trapped inside the 13th Dimension," Aries continues, "and I'm going to get him out."

Say what? I'm in total shock. Two minutes ago, I thought we were getting off of this planet to avoid going into the 13th Dimension! Now, he's telling me he wants to go inside the 13th Dimension voluntarily! Is he nuts?

"Sorry," I say. "But how do you know he's actually in there?"

"Because he haunts me in my nightmares," Aries says matter-of-factly. "He comes to me every night, begging for my help."

For a second, I'm speechless.

I mean, is he serious?

"Um," I say, "are you sure about this? I mean, everyone has bad dreams now and then. I have a recurring nightmare where my sister is the leader of the Freedom Force, but I know it's not true."

"I understand your skepticism," he says. "But I'm certain he's reaching out to me. Look, I won't tell you what I had to do to get the Paladins to lock me up here. But now that I'm here, I'm not turning back."

He looks so determined I can't deny he believes it.

But do I?

"We fought together as teammates on Arena World," Aries says. "Will you join me in my quest to save Wind Walker?"

As I look into his brown eyes, they flicker with a strange blue energy. But just as quickly, it's gone.

That's weird. Am I imagining things now?

"Well?" Aries asks.

I take a deep breath. I mean, I could never walk away if Wind Walker needed my help, no matter how crazy the circumstances.

"Of course I'll help," I say, shocked to hear my own words. "But how do we get inside?"

As Aries looks up, I feel like a bonehead.

The Cosmic Key!

"Stop them!" comes a voice.

I turn to find hundreds of bright lights in the sky.

The Paladins!

RRIIIIPPPP!

I look back over at Aries who is now holding the huge, gray disc. Peering down, I'm suddenly staring into a swirling abyss of purple energy.

It's the 13th Dimension!

"Grab the Cosmic Key!" Aries yells.

What? The last time I touched a cosmic entity, I couldn't get rid of it!

"Now!" he yells. Then, he tosses the gray disc like a Frisbee, striking the black cube so hard it splits in half, exposing the Cosmic Key above us.

"Halt!" a Paladin yells.

They're nearly on top of us! I don't have time to grab the Key now, even if I tried!

So instead, I go to plan B.

I concentrate hard, pushing my energy towards the Cosmic Key. Then, I pull it back in and the power surge hits me like a Mack truck.

There's a tremendous rush of power.

Like my body feels electric.

But it's more power than I can contain.

"Q-Quick!" I stammer, reaching out. "Grab me!"

I feel him wrap his large hand around mine, and then we jump into the circle of nebulous purple energy, slipping like ghosts into the 13th Dimension.

Meta Profile

Xenox

Name: Xenox Xanth	Height: 5'10"
Race: Unknown	Weight: 163 lbs
Status: Villain/Active	Eyes/Hair: Red/Bald

META 0: No Powers	Observed Characteristics	
Lieutenant in Krule the Conqueror's Motley Crew	Combat 18	
	Durability 21	Leadership 43
Superior Pilot	Strategy 65	Willpower 51

SIX

I HATE THE NUMBER THIRTEEN

It's funny how your mind wanders when you're falling to your doom.

I mean, even though I'm plunging into the 13th Dimension, strangely, all I'm thinking about is how I could use a vacation right now. From what I've heard, most kids get to go on a few cool vacations, like Disney World, the Grand Canyon, or Niagara Falls.

But me? No siree Bob.

According to Mom and Dad, superheroes don't take vacations. Instead, we're supposed to be on call all the time. You know, just in case the world needs saving.

I get it, but don't superheroes deserve a break too? I know we do exciting work, but I'd trade relaxing on a beach for falling into the 13th Dimension any day of the week.

But I'm not sure Aries would agree with me. Based on his steely expression, he looks like he's actually excited to enter the 13th Dimension. Which is impressive because I'm downright terrified!

I mean, what are we thinking? Aries said he's sure Wind Walker is in the 13th Dimension, but what if he's wrong? Then we just dove in here for nothing!

But I guess it's my fault we're in this situation to begin with. Instead of absorbing the power of the Cosmic Key, I could have just let the Paladins capture us. I'm guessing that would have been a lot less painful than whatever's waiting for us when we hit the bottom of this thing.

If we ever hit the bottom of this thing.

It feels like we've been falling through purplish matter forever, but suddenly we break into a thick layer of gray fog. I'm still holding Aries' hand, but I can't see him anymore! I'm about to call out when we enter a beige sky and then—

"Oof!" I exclaim, slamming into something hard.

Aries and I disconnect, and my back is killing me from whatever I just smashed into, but I don't have time to lick my wounds because I'm suddenly tumbling down a rocky mountainside! I'm picking up speed fast, but there's nothing to grab to slow my fall. All I can do is shield my head as my body fumbles end-over-end like a football until I finally hit the bottom. A plume of dirt kicks up into the air and lands back on my face.

I sit up, spitting out a mouthful.

Just. Freaking. Wonderful.

"Are you okay?" Aries asks, standing heroically in front of me like he just stepped out of a toothpaste commercial.

"Yeah," I say, wiping my chin. "Did that rock monster nail you too?"

"No," he says. "I landed on a sand dune."

"Of course you did," I mutter, getting to my feet. "Where are we anyway?"

"Somewhere in the 13th Dimension I presume," he says. "If we're going to find Wind Walker, we'd better move fast. The longer we stay out in the open like this, the easier a target we'll become."

Speaking of out in the open, all I see is desert for miles around, but it's not smooth and flat. The terrain varies widely, with dips and valleys offset by the occasional sand dune. Way off in the distance are giant, craggy mountains, like the one I crashed into.

Great. The 13th Dimension is a giant wasteland.

I shiver. And boy, it's cold. Then I look up and realize there's no sun. That gray fog blankets the entire sky. And there's a strange black dot moving—

Suddenly, Aries grabs me and pulls me against the mountain.

"Hey!" I say, "why'd you—"

"Shhh!" he whispers.

When I look back up, I realize he's right. That little black dot has become a large black creature, with giant wings and a long tail. Thankfully, it doesn't seem like it noticed us, but it's looping around in circles.

We stay still for what seems like an eternity until the creature finally disappears.

"Okay," I say, "how about we speed this rescue thing up? Did Wind Walker tell you where to find him? Because there's pretty much a whole lot of nothing in every direction."

"No," Aries says. "This is going to be a huge guessing game. Maybe there's a landmark or something I'll recognize."

"You mean, like her?" I ask.

I do a double take because standing behind Aries is an old woman who simply wasn't there before. She's hunched over, wearing a black robe with a hood that covers most of her face, except for her hooked nose and blue eyes. Her very, very alert-looking blue eyes.

"Who are you?" Aries asks, taking a step backward.

"Well, I should ask the same of you, shouldn't I?" she says, with an unnerving smirk.

"We're just passing through," he says. "Our names aren't important."

"Yes, names aren't important, are they?" she says, waving dismissively. Then she looks at Aries and says, "My what large horns you have." Then, she looks down at me and says "And you are but a child. It is so rare to find a child here. Did you just arrive?"

"Yes," Aries says.

"Oh, you poor, unfortunate souls," she says, sympathetically. "I've lost a bit of hearing in my old age, but did you just say you were passing through? If so, I'm sorry to tell you that those who enter the realm can never leave."

"The realm?" I ask.

"Oh, yes," she says, with a sweep of her arm. "This is the realm. And those who enter never leave. Unless, of course, you know of a way out?"

Aries and I look at one another and I swallow hard.

No, we don't know a way out. I mean, I didn't have time to grab the Cosmic Key like Aries asked, and I don't feel its power inside of me anymore. Plus, we've fallen so far from Paladin Planet I couldn't duplicate it again if I tried. Now we'll be stuck here… forever.

"I thought as much," she sighs, her crooked body deflating. "I always ask anyone new if they know how to get out. I've been here for so long it would be nice to escape this drab world and allow these weary bones to finally expire somewhere more colorful."

For a second, she looks so sad I feel bad for her. But then I realize I can't let my guard down. I mean, we're in the freaking 13th Dimension! If this grandma is stuck here, I'm guessing it's for a good reason.

"Well," she says. "Perhaps I could offer you some help? I know so much about the realm. Oh, I used to be so good at helping."

"And what would you want in exchange for that help?" Aries asks.

"Oh, nothing," she says. "Nothing at all. Helping is a reward in itself. My father used to say that. Once upon a time I so enjoyed being helpful. But no one seems to want my help anymore. It's a shame really. I can be very helpful if I want to be. Very helpful indeed."

Aries looks at me and I nod.

"Okay," he says. "We're looking for someone."

"Aren't we all?" she says glumly. "But isn't it always the case that when you're most in search of a friend, none can be found?"

"Well," I say, "We're looking for—"

"Yes, friends are hard to find," Aries says, cutting me off and throwing me a look that says 'stop-talking.' "Tell me, who is in charge of the realm?"

Huh? Why'd he interrupt me like that?

"Oh, ho, ho," she snickers, wringing her hands. "Cutting to the chase, aren't you? Yes, the realm always has a ruler. Especially of late. First, there was Broote the Barbaric. But he was dethroned."

"Broote?" Aries says, his voice rising. "Broote is here? In the realm?"

"Um, who is Broote?" I ask.

"Later," Aries says. "So, tell me, who is powerful enough to dethrone the mighty Broote?"

"A man of three eyes," she says. "He was known as

Krule. Krule the—"

"—Conqueror!" I blurt out.

"Yes," she says. "Krule the Conqueror drove Broote from power and ruled the realm with an iron fist. But he and his army have gone missing."

Missing?

Okay, I know for sure Krule isn't missing. He somehow escaped from the 13th Dimension by getting the Cosmic Key. But maybe she doesn't know that. Well, I'm certainly not gonna tell her.

"Hold on," Aries says. "So, if Krule is missing why isn't Broote back in power?"

"Because there is another," she says. "And he is even more powerful. Very powerful indeed."

"And does this powerful man have a name?" I ask.

"As you said, names aren't important," she says. "But as the ruler of the realm he demands to be called 'King,' and all must bow down before him. If you refuse, he can be quite ruthless—more ruthless than even Krule. But the King knows everything about the realm and its inhabitants. Maybe even more than me."

"And where can we find this King?" Aries asks.

"Well, isn't it obvious?" she says. "The King is in the castle. Aren't all Kings in a castle?"

I look around, but I don't see any castles towering over the horizon.

"Oh, you will not see the castle like that," she says like she's reading my mind. "This castle is underground."

Underground?

Seriously?

"Would you like me to take you there?" she asks. "I can be very helpful if I want to be."

"Um, no thanks," Aries says. "But maybe you could point us in the right direction?"

"Oh, I do enjoy being helpful," she says. Then, she spins around three times, finally stopping with her arm pointed towards the biggest mountain on the horizon. "It is that way. You must pass through the Narrow Chasm and the entrance will be just on the other side. But be careful, there are those here who will try to harm you. Oh, and there is something else. But no, I mustn't. Please forgive me, there is a child present. Maybe I should…"

"Wait," I say. "What is it?"

"Oh, no, I don't want to upset you any further," she says, backing up. "I have so enjoyed being helpful."

"It's okay," Aries says. "He can take it. You've been very helpful so far. We would appreciate any additional help."

"You would?" she says, her eyes widening. "Oh, well that's wonderful."

"Yes," I say. "Please."

"Very well," she says, her eyes narrowing, "you should know that something else lives in the realm. Something evil."

A chill runs down my spine.

"It is known only as 'the Shadow,'" she continues.

"It has lived in the realm since the very beginning—seeing all, hearing all, understanding all. It is ever-present. And it is waiting."

"Um, waiting for what?" I ask.

"For its chance to escape," she says.

Okay, now I'm creeped out.

"Thanks for your ghost story," Aries says quickly. "But we're going to head off now."

"Oh, of course," she says frowning. "I... I... understand. Shame on me. Sometimes I can be too helpful. Remember to follow the Narrow Chasm and be very, very careful. I wish you all the best in finding your friend Wind Walker."

I look at Aries.

D-Did she just say Wind Walker?

How'd she know we were looking for Wind Walker?

We never mentioned his name.

But when I turn back to ask her, she's gone.

Meta Profile

Aries

⬚ Name: Ramm V'kkar	⬚ Height: 6'5"
⬚ Race: Ani-man	⬚ Weight: 325 lbs
⬚ Status: Hero/Active	⬚ Eyes/Hair: Brown/Bald

META 3: Super-Strength	Observed Characteristics	
⬚ Extreme Strength	Combat 100	
⬚ Extreme invulnerability	Durability 100	Leadership 62
⬚ Extreme Power Charge	Strategy 65	Willpower 95

SEVEN

I MIGHT BE CRAZY

We've been wandering in the desert for hours.

Or at least it feels like hours because I can't tell what time it is. Apparently, there's no way of knowing whether it's day or night in the 13th Dimension because every time I look at the sky it's always the same color—dull gray.

I'm also starting to think the mountain that old woman directed us towards is one big mirage because no matter how far I think we've traveled, it never seems to get any closer. It's like we're walking aimlessly on some invisible treadmill, racking up tons of miles without really getting anywhere.

Truthfully, I'm not sure how much longer I can go on. My legs are aching and if we don't find this Narrow Chasm soon, I'm gonna collapse. Aries, however, looks like he could run a marathon.

Maybe he's saving his energy by not talking to me.

I mean, I tried making conversation, but he just doesn't seem interested. And it's not like we don't have a lot of things to talk about. The last time I heard his voice was when I asked him why he cut me off in our conversation with the old woman.

"I got a bad vibe," he said. "When I told her we were looking for *someone*, she knew we were looking for a *friend*. That made me suspicious."

"Okay," I said. "I get it now. And what do you think about that 'Shadow' business? Do you really think there's some evil force out there?"

"Nope," he answered.

And that was it.

It's been radio silence ever since.

Which is a shame because I've been dying to learn more about that Broote guy. I'd love to know why Aries was so alarmed when the old woman mentioned his name. I've never heard of 'Broote the Barbaric' before, but Aries clearly has, and he didn't seem happy about it.

Since Aries wouldn't answer my straightforward questions, I tried approaching the subject more subtly. Like: "I bet that Broote guy owes you a lot of money, right?" Or: "Hey, I forgot, was that guy's name Broote or Boot?"

Okay, maybe that last one wasn't so subtle.

But no matter what angle I took, Aries wouldn't bite.

So, I tried changing the subject to stuff we have in common, like our mutual friends on the Zodiac. After all, I'd love to know what the old gang was up to—including Gemini. Well, especially Gemini. But when I asked him about the team, he didn't respond either.

What's with him?

But even though he's been quiet, my mind hasn't stopped spinning. I mean, how did that old woman know we were looking for Wind Walker anyway? It doesn't make sense. Neither of us mentioned his name. I'd say she was a Psychic, except for the fact that Meta powers don't work in the 13th Dimension.

So, what gives?

Not that I have the brainpower to figure it out right now. At this point, I'm hungry and delirious. I wipe my bleary eyes when Aries whispers—

"Hit the deck!"

His words sound like sweet music to my ears, and I drop to the ground like an anchor, happy to be off of my feet. We're lying on the side of a sand dune and I'm wondering if my cape would make a serviceable pillow when I look up and freeze.

That's when I realize Aries isn't stopping for a rest.

Someone is running right towards us.

My heart skips a beat for two reasons.

First, the man heading our way has blue skin like Wind Walker, and for a split second, I think we're the luckiest fools alive. But then I realize he's bald and way too tall to be Wind Walker. Second, the guy is yelling at the top of his lungs. And what he's saying gives me pause.

"Stay away!" he screams. "Leave me alone!"

He's hightailing it like he's being chased by a pack of wolves. But the thing is, there's no one behind him.

"Stay low and go to the other side," Aries whispers.

I nod, my heart beating a mile a minute. As I shift over, I keep my head below the top of the dunes so I can't be seen. But when I look at Aries, he's crawling into the center, directly in the guy's path!

He's going to intercept him!

"Stay back!" the man yells.

Although I can't see him, I can hear him getting closer. I swallow hard. I mean, is tackling this guy a good idea? This would be our first real fight down here. And without our powers who knows what could happen?

Suddenly, a figure leaps over the dune.

And that's when Aries pounces!

"Ugh!" the man exclaims, as Aries slams into him.

They roll down the side of the dune, a tangle of arms and legs. I want to help Aries, but first I can't help peeking over the dunes to take a look around. I scan the barren wasteland, looking for any sign of movement, but I still don't see anything. There's absolutely no one coming. Then, the sounds of Aries and the man scuffling snap me back to reality.

By the time I slide down the dune on my derriere, Aries has done all of the hard work. He has the man pinned, lying face-down on his stomach with his arms pulled behind his back.

Now, Aries is a tall dude but this guy is even taller—like, pro-basketball-player-tall. And he's breathing hard like Aries knocked the wind out of him. I kneel to ask him what his deal is when he suddenly turns his head to face me and our eyes meet.

My jaw drops.

I'd know those cat-like eyes anywhere.

This isn't just any tall guy.

It's the Overlord!

Instinctively, I spring to my feet. I mean, the Overlord is a major Meta 3 villain who can control gravity! My stomach turns just thinking about what he did to us back on the Ghost Ship. How come I didn't recognize him? Then, I realize he's not wearing his helmet.

"Be careful," I warn Aries. "That's—"

"—the Overlord," Aries says. "Yeah, I know. I was on Arena World too. Fortunately, he's powerless down here."

Speaking of Arena World, the last time I saw the Overlord, he was operating as one of Chaos' combatants in pursuit of the Building Block. How the heck did he get down here? He must have escaped Arena World before the whole planet exploded. I guess the Paladins picked him up at some point and threw him in here.

"Let me go!" he demands, his eyes wild with panic.

"They'll catch me! I can't let them catch me!"

"Relax, big guy," Aries says. "There's no one following you."

"You idiots!" the Overlord says, his eyebrows raised. "They're right there! Don't you see them? They're floating right there!"

Aries and I both look up to the top of the dune, but there's nothing there. Not a person. Not a floating thing.

Nothing.

What's going on? He's not making any sense. But then it dawns on me.

Maybe he's crazy.

I mean, this place could make anyone crazy.

"I hear you," I say calmly. "But we can't see them right now so maybe you can fill us in. Who, or what, is chasing you?"

"The Wraiths!" he says. "They scour the realm looking for hosts to possess. They have no bodies of their own, and if they catch you, they'll take over your soul!"

"Well, that does sound disturbing," I say.

"Do not mock me," the Overlord says. "I can tell you don't believe me. But you'll see."

"Okay," I say. "So, tell us. Where did these, um, Wraith-thingies come from?"

"The castle," the Overlord says. "They came from the castle."

"The castle?" I say. "You don't mean the underground castle, do you?"

"It's haunted," he says. "Cursed!"

Right.

Of course it is.

"I just want to go home," he babbles, tears running down his cheeks. "Please, I just want to go home."

I'm taken aback. I mean, not too long ago, the Overlord was one of the most feared crime lords in the galaxy. And now he's a driveling mess.

"So," I ask Aries. "What do we do with him now?"

"Now?" Aries says. "We let him go. We can't take him with us, and I don't think he's in any state to provide useful information anyway."

"Yes, let me go," the Overlord begs. "Please, I'm not useful. I must go. They're… they're coming!"

"Get lost," Aries says, releasing the Overlord.

"Get away from me!" the villain yells, springing to his feet. As he bolts, he screams, "Leave me alone! Please, leave me alone!"

"Let's go," Aries says, walking the opposite way.

But as I watch the Overlord disappear into the distance, shouting and flailing his arms, I get a terrible thought.

If this place can turn one of the most dangerous villains in the multiverse into that, who's to say it won't happen to us?

I catch up with Aries.

"Hey," I say. "You don't think that thing he said about the Wraiths is—"

"No," Aries says, cutting me off. "I don't."

But as we walk across the sand in silence, I'm not so sure.

Meta Profile

The Overlord

Name: Unknown	Height: 6'9"
Race: Dhoom	Weight: 546 lbs
Status: Villain/Inactive	Eyes/Hair: Yellow/Bald

META 0: No Powers	Observed Characteristics	
Former Crime Boss	Combat 35	
Prisoner in the 13th Dimension	Durability 30	Leadership 22
Powers have been negated	Strategy 24	Willpower 5

EIGHT

I GRAB THE BULL BY THE HORNS

Our prospects seem to be dimming by the second.

We're still wandering aimlessly through the desert, we have no idea when we'll stumble across the Narrow Chasm, and we have no clue how we'll get out of here even if we find Wind Walker.

That pretty much makes us 0 for 3.

One big strikeout.

Not to mention our encounter with the Overlord is still freaking me out. I mean, I simply can't match up the person I just saw with the person I once knew. Somehow, this place turned him from a major powerhouse into a hopeless wreck.

Not to mention that thing he said about the Wraiths.

I shudder.

The faster we finish this mission the better.

The problem is, we don't seem to be getting very far. It's like we're walking in ultra-slow motion without even knowing it. I stare at my feet. They're definitely moving.

At least, it seems like they're moving.

Suddenly, Aries stops and says, "We're here."

Huh?

When I look up, I realize we're standing in the shadow of a giant mountain. Wait a second, how'd that happen? A minute ago, we were miles away. Did some invisible hand pick us up and drop us here in the blink of an eye?

This is too weird.

Something isn't right.

But before I can figure it out, Aries points to the center of the mountain and says, "There."

Zeroing in, I notice a sliver of light running north to south down the middle of the rock monolith. At first, I'm not sure what it is, but then I realize it's a jagged fissure, letting light through from the other side.

What is that?

Then it hits me.

It's the Narrow Chasm!

We found it! I reach up for a high five but I'm left hanging because Aries is already gone, running towards it.

Well, that was awkward.

I sprint to catch up, and as I reach the base of the mountain I marvel at the natural wonder before me. It's like someone took a knife and cut straight through the mountain itself like it was a seven-layer cake. And I can see how it got its name because the chasm itself is narrow alright. I watch Aries turn himself sideways and wedge himself in, tilting his head up to prevent his horns from scraping the other side. Then, he's off.

I'm not sure where this thing lets out, but it's not like I'm planning on waiting here for him to ring me when he gets to the other side. So, I take a deep breath and follow. Fortunately, this is one time it pays to be small because I've got plenty of elbow room.

We make our way through slowly, but it's not exactly smooth sailing. While the chasm is open to the sky, it's definitely darker at the bottom versus the top. Plus, there are plenty of spots where the mountain juts out and we have to maneuver ourselves either over or under to keep going. At one point, my concentration lapses, and I nearly eat a face full of rock.

But hopefully, all of this effort will be worth it, because the old woman said the entrance to the underground castle is just on the other side of this mountain. Supposedly, that's where we'll meet the King who may be our only shot at finding Wind Walker.

Unless, of course, she was misleading us.

Regardless, I'll be happy to reach the end. Tight spaces like this just aren't my jam. Once, Dog-Gone and I snuck out of bed for a midnight snack and got stuck hiding in the pantry for two hours until Dad finished a late dinner. That wasn't fun, especially since I had to give my snack to Dog-Gone just to keep him quiet. Boy, I'd give anything to be back in the pantry with that mutt again.

Just thinking about him makes my eyes well up.

But as much as I miss him, I need to stay focused.

This chasm goes on forever, but I have to admit, it does make a perfect secret passageway.

"We've reached the end," Aries says suddenly.

What? Yes!

I look up just as he squeezes through the final section and pops out the other side. Light streams in and my heart swells with joy. I skip gleefully out of the Narrow Chasm, hop over a pile of rocks, and SLAM into the muscular leg of a very large man, bouncing me onto my backside.

Ouch! And who is that?

I take in the figure of the man I crashed into. He's big and muscular and wearing a black costume with the insignia of a ram on his chest. But that's not all. He has two large horns protruding from his forehead—just like Aries!

Just then, two other lunkheads step out of the shadows behind us, blocking any escape back through the Narrow Chasm.

We're trapped!

"Broote," Aries says.

My jaw hits the floor.

Broote? That's Broote?

"Little brother," Broote says, with a menacing grin.

My jaw hits the floor again.

Did he just call Aries... brother?

"I never expected to find you here," Broote says. "What happened? Did you get caught stealing someone's lunch credits?"

"Step aside, Broote," Aries says. "I'm on an important mission. I don't have time for you."

"You haven't changed at all, have you?" Broote asks, cracking his ginormous knuckles. "Still the arrogant fool. You may not have time for me, but I have plenty of time for you."

"I'm warning you, brother," Aries says, the veins on his neck bulging. "We aren't in the coliseum anymore, and you aren't half the gladiator you think you are."

"You're partially correct," Broote says, looking around. "This isn't the coliseum, but unfortunately for you, I'm still twice the gladiator you'll ever be. This should be fun. And to think, I haven't had a good battle since Ravager destroyed our homeworld and all of the people you once loved."

"Like our parents?" Aries yells, his face flushed. "You couldn't rule our world, so you sold it out to Ravager like the traitor you are. You betrayed everyone out of spite. All you ever craved was power and look what it got you. No wonder father never loved you."

"Perhaps he didn't," Broote says casually. "But I'm

alive and he's dead. So, guess who is on top now?"

"Fool," Aries scoffs. "You call this living? You're a shell of your former self, trapped in a prison you can't escape from. You're so pathetic you can't even hold the throne of this wasteland."

"Don't belittle me, brother," Broote says. "If you consider me a failure then what are you? I watched you try to avenge our people against Ravager—failing time and time again—until Ravager was destroyed, but not at your hand." Then, he looks at me and says, "You needed this child to do the job. You're pathetic."

Hang on. If Broote was stuck here in the 13th Dimension, then how did he see me beat Ravager? It doesn't make sense.

"Enough!" Aries yells. "Perhaps I have time for you after all. Maybe we were destined to meet again. Maybe it's time for you to pay your debt to our people—to our parents—once and for all."

"That's the spirit," Broote says. "Soldiers, subdue my brother's pet. I will deal with him after I've won."

Pet? What pet? Wait, is he talking about—

"Hey!" I yell as the two goons grab my arms!

I try pulling myself free but it's useless, they're too strong. But when I look back over, Aries and Broote are facing off, measuring each other as they walk in a slow, deliberate circle.

"This ends here," Aries says.

"Correction," Broote replies. "You end here."

OMG!

They're going to fight each other!

To the death!

Then, before I can blink, the brothers charge one another with their horns out first, just like rams!

CRASH!

Their collision kicks up a massive dust cloud that covers everything. Instinctively, I shut my eyes, protecting them from the storm. When the dust finally settles, the brothers are locked in close combat, their arms and horns interlocked! The two warriors push against one another, trying to use their horns as leverage to knock the other off balance. Suddenly, Broote finds an opening and delivers a swift uppercut to Aries' jaw, sending him flying into the side of the mountain.

"Still falling for that one, brother?" Broote says. "A shame. I wonder, will you beg for mercy?"

"I don't beg," Aries says, spitting out blood as he rises to his feet. "Never have, never will."

Then, Aries charges again and Broote lowers his horns just in time. My ears ring as the two collide once again, pushing against each other with all of their might. This time, Broote sweeps Aries' right leg and pummels him with a roundhouse kick, sending Aries stumbling to the ground.

This is not good.

Aries is a great fighter, but Broote is even better! If this is going to the death, Aries doesn't stand a chance!

"Do you want to continue, brother?" Broote says, a smug expression on his face. "Or would you rather surrender to the inevitable?"

Without a word, Aries rises to his feet.

But this time there's something different about him.

His eyes...

They're flickering again with that strange blue energy. Just like I saw before!

"What are you doing?" Broote asks.

"Enough distractions," Aries says, his eyes flaring. "You are keeping me from my goal."

Suddenly, Aries morphs into a gray blur, and there's an ear-splitting BOOM that rattles my teeth. The next thing I know, I'm engulfed in an even bigger dust cloud that makes my eyes water.

The goons drop me to the ground, and I rub my eyes to clear the sting. But when I can finally see again, Aries is standing in Broote's spot, and there's a massive hole in the side of the mountain itself.

Where's Broote?

Then, I see a limp, black-costumed body lying inside the hole. It's Broote! But what happened?

And then I realize...

Aries has Meta powers!

Aries turns and my former captors take off through the Narrow Chasm. Aries rubs his eyes, and when he's finished, they're brown again.

"What happened?" he asks.

"What happened?" I repeat. "You just used your Meta powers to pummel Broote. Don't you remember?"

"Broote?" he says, and then he sees his brother's body. He runs over and hops inside the hole. Kneeling, he checks Broote's pulse and then closes his sibling's eyes.

"Is he...?" I ask.

"Yes," Aries says, coming back out. "He's gone."

"I'm sorry," I say. "But how did that even happen? I thought you couldn't use Meta powers in the 13th Dimension? I thought everyone here lived forever?"

"I... I don't know," Aries says.

Aries looks at his brother's body and lowers his head.

"Are you okay?" I ask.

"Yes," he says. "I did what needed to be done. I just don't remember doing it."

"You mean, you seriously don't remember?"

"No," he says. "I have no memory of what happened."

Wow, that's scary.

"Do you need a minute?" I ask.

"No," he says. "Broote finally got what he deserved. But this doesn't change why we came here. We need to resume our mission. We need to find the underground castle and see if this 'King' knows where we can find Wind Walker."

I nod and we both start scanning the area for an entrance, but there aren't any obvious openings anywhere. What did that old woman say? Something about it being just on the other side of the Narrow Chasm? But where?

Wait a second, 'just on the other side?'

I run over to the Narrow Chasm and look straight down. Sure enough, that pile of rocks I jumped over doesn't look like an ordinary pile of rocks.

There's thirteen of them. And they're arranged in a perfect circle. That can't be a coincidence.

"Aries!" I call out. "I think I found something!"

"That's got to be it," he says, checking it out.

"It's something," I say. "But I don't get why these rocks are arranged in a circle."

"Because it's not a circle," he says. "It's an entrance."

An entrance? But there's just dirt inside?

"Really?" he says. "Follow me."

Then, he hops into the center and disappears!

Oh, jeez, he's right! That circle must be an illusion!

But before I step inside, I hesitate. I mean, why do I keep ending up going underground?

I hate going underground!

But what other choice do I have?

So, I pinch my nose, close my eyes, and jump into the center of the circle.

Meta Profile

Broote

Name: Kole V'kkar	Height: 6'7"
Race: Ani-man	Weight: 355 lbs
Status: Villain/Inactive	Eyes/Hair: Brown/Bald

META 0: No Powers	Observed Characteristics	
Former villain	Combat 62	
Prisoner in the 13th Dimension	Durability 65	Leadership 60
Powers have been negated	Strategy 61	Willpower 97

NINE

I HAVE AN AUDIENCE WITH THE KING

I'm lying face down on a cold, stone floor.

The good news is that I'm alive. The bad news is that I've got no clue how long I've been lying here.

The last thing I remember is jumping into the middle of that rock ring and sliding down a rampway so steep I thought I was going to pass out. I guess I did.

Even though everything feels like it's spinning, I get up onto my hands and knees to take a look around, but it's pitch dark.

Then I realize my cape is flipped over my head.

Genius.

After handling that little embarrassment, the room isn't nearly as dark as I thought, because there's a torch flickering on the far wall giving off some light. From what I can gather, I'm in a small room with rock walls and a high ceiling. Looking up, I see the end of a stone ramp some ten feet off the ground. Well, if that's where I got off, I'm lucky I'm not dead right now.

I bet Aries stuck his landing like an Olympic gymnast. Speaking of Aries, where is the big lug? I mean, I thought we were going to tackle this underground castle together.

Then, I notice an empty torch bracket on the wall.

I'm guessing Aries took that one.

So, where'd he go?

I pull the remaining torch off the wall and wave it around. There must be a passageway around here somewhere? It takes me a little while, but I finally find it.

Tucked in the corner is a creepy stone stairway headed straight down.

Wonderful.

With torch in hand, I descend slowly, the air getting mustier with every step. I do my best not to make any noise, but it's so deathly quiet I'm nervous to even breathe!

As I go down the stairs, I notice strange symbols carved into the wall. They look like Egyptian hieroglyphics, but I can't make out what they mean. What I can tell, however, is that this certainly isn't the vibe I was expecting when I heard the word 'castle.' I mean, where are all of the knights and flowery tapestries?

I step onto a stone landing that connects to another chamber that's slightly larger than the one above. There are all kinds of weapons spilled on the floor, like axes, spears, and swords. By the looks of it, I'm guessing this was a guard post. Thankfully, it's unmanned, but what happened to all of the guards?

Suddenly, I think of the Overlord.

Did the Wraiths get them?

The stairway continues so I go down another level where I find an even larger chamber, but there's still no one around. This one has a bunch of busted open crates filled with ropes and nails and other building supplies. And it's the same story for level four, level five, and so on. The chambers keep getting larger, but more eerily empty.

This is not comforting.

And where's Aries? I never thought he'd leave me behind like this. I want to call out his name, but I don't exactly want to announce I'm here. So, my only option is to just keep looking.

By the time I reach the twelfth level my legs are killing me. Note to self: do more Stairmaster work in the gym. Again, there's no one around. Then, I look down and feel a pit in my stomach.

The stairway ends at the bottom of the next level.

Level thirteen.

Yep, I should've predicted that.

I take a deep breath. If the King is here, I'm guessing

that's where I'm gonna find him. I lean forward, listening for any noise, but it's deathly quiet.

No King. No Aries. No nothing.

Truthfully, I'm totally spooked right now. It feels like I'm walking through one of those Halloween haunted house tours where you just know something is going to jump out and scare the pants off of you.

Except those are fake. This is all too real.

My brain is telling me to run back up these stairs to safety as quickly as possible, but deep down I know I can't. Wind Walker needs my help. And by the looks of it, so does Aries.

I take a deep breath and head down the final flight of stairs. I've got to be ready for anything, so when I reach the bottom step I leap off and assume a fighting stance, but thankfully there's no one around.

But this time there's no chamber.

Instead, there's a corridor.

A corridor lined with lit torches.

Which can only mean one thing.

Someone is down here!

I hesitate. I mean, who knows what's waiting for me at the end of this corridor? And without Aries or my powers, I'll be in deep trouble if I run into something I can't handle. But I've come too far to turn back now.

I walk slowly, curiosity propelling me forward.

Of course, didn't curiosity kill the cat?

As I reach the end of the corridor, I can see it opens

into a large, circular room. I press my back against the wall and peek inside the door-less frame.

The room is empty, except for a massive crystal sitting in its center! It's purple in color—like an amethyst—but it must be six-feet tall. The front and back are perfectly flat, like the surface of a mirror, while the perimeter is hexagonal.

It's so remarkable I can't take my eyes away.

Without thinking, I find myself walking right up to it. Off to the side is a torch holder, so I set mine inside, leaving both hands free. I stand in front of the crystal, dwarfed by its sheer size. It's only when I'm this close that I realize it's translucent. I reach around and see my hand on the other side. Boy, I bet this baby would fetch big bucks back on Earth.

Instinctively, I reach out and touch it, pressing my palm against the surface. Suddenly, the face of the crystal goes from clear to a dark, swirling mist—and the next thing I know, I'm staring at Dog-Gone's big behind!

Shocked, I pull my hand away and Dog-Gone disappears. Huh? What's going on?

But when I touch the crystal again, Dog-Gone is back. And he's sitting in the Mission Room of the Waystation. Then, everything clicks.

Broote said he was watching me defeat Ravager even though he was trapped in the 13th Dimension. Could he have been using this crystal to do it? Because if what I'm seeing is real, it's like looking through a window into another world!

I keep my left hand on the surface and knock on the face of the crystal with my right, but Dog-Gone doesn't react. Instead, he seems really focused chewing away on something. Wait a minute, that's my slipper!

"Hey!" I yell, banging hard against the crystal. "Drop my slipper you stupid mutt!"

Suddenly, Dog-Gone lifts his head.

OMG! Can he hear me?

"Here, boy!" I yell. "I'm over here!"

Dog-Gone spins around confused.

I can't believe it! I think he can hear me!

"Come on, buddy!" I yell, waving frantically. "It's me, Elliott! I'm standing right here! I need help!"

Dog-Gone stops and sniffs the air like he senses me, but I don't think he can actually see me.

"Get help, boy," I yell. "Get Mom or Dad! Get TechnocRat or Makeshift! Well, don't get Makeshift, but get someone! And fast!"

But instead of following directions, he sits down and wags his tail from side-to-side.

Clearly, he ain't no Lassie.

"Dog-Gone, no!" I yell, pounding on the crystal. "Bad dog! Go get help! Get off your rump and get—"

But just like that, he's gone!

The surface of the crystal turns murky again, and when it settles, I found myself staring at a control panel.

What the—? Where am I?

Then, I look up through a windshield at outer space. Dead center is a large red planet with green rings around it. At first, I think it's Saturn, but Saturn isn't red.

"We are close, Commander," comes a voice to my left.

I turn to find an alien with white skin and big red eyes staring at me. He looks just like Xenox, except it's not Xenox because this guy is just as ugly but way fatter.

"As expected, they have deployed their armada," the alien continues. "We expect the first wave to arrive in twenty point two seconds. Shall we ready the torpedoes?"

"Prepare them, Lieutenant," comes a deep, strangely familiar voice. "But hold fire until I can see the neon green of their eyes."

That voice? I feel like I've heard it before.

But from where?

Suddenly, a huge, red-skinned figure comes into view, and the hairs on the back of my neck stand on end.

OMG!

It's... Krule the Conqueror!

And he's like, eight feet tall!

"First, I will destroy their army," Krule says, grinning from ear to ear. "Then, I will capture their homeworld. And last but not least, I will destroy their Emperor!"

Emperor?

As in, the Skelton Emperor?

"Enemy warships in sight," the Lieutenant says.

"Wait for my command," Krule orders.

Just then, hundreds of Skelton warships appear.

They're coming in fast, getting closer. What's he waiting for? Suddenly, I see the face of the lead Skelton pilot. He's heading straight for the bridge!

He's going to ram us!

But then, the pilot's eyes turn an even brighter shade of green and he veers off at the last second, followed by ship after Skelton ship! What's going on?

I watch as the first wave of Skelton ships loop behind the second wave—and begin firing!

They're blowing up their own ships!

How is that happening?

But when I look over at Krule I have my answer. His third eye is glowing with a strong green light. He's mind-controlling them! He's using Skelton ships to destroy their own army!

"I'm coming for you, old friend," Krule says. "And just like I warned you, the final laugh will be mine."

Then, the whole scene disappears.

I stagger backward, my adrenaline pumping.

That was nuts! Krule is trying to take over the Skelton Homeworld!

I'm about to reach for the crystal again when I notice something out of the corner of my eye. There's a bright light coming from an open doorway that simply wasn't there before.

Was it triggered when I touched the crystal?

This time I leave my torch behind and duck into the

shadows. I inch my way over to the opening, walking as softly as possible. When I reach the doorway, I press my ear to the wall.

I don't hear anything, but that doesn't mean there's nothing in there. And if there is something in there it certainly knows I'm here. After all, I *was* yelling at the top of my lungs for Dog-Gone to get help. It's amazing how that pooch gets me in trouble, even out here.

But honestly, I'm sick and tired of tiptoeing around. If I'm going down, I'd rather do it in a blaze of glory. So, here goes nothing.

One… Two…

Three! I jump through the entrance in karate-chop mode, ready for action! But no one attacks. Instead, there's a large, gold throne sitting in the center of the room, facing the other way. And standing stock-still by its side is Aries!

"Bow before the King," Aries orders.

"Excuse me?" I say. Then, I notice his eyes are sparking with that strange blue energy again.

"Bow before the King," Aries repeats.

Suddenly, the throne swivels, revealing a blue-skinned man wearing a crown on his head!

My heart skips a beat.

I-I can't believe it. It's the King!

But the King is… Wind Walker?

TEN

I CAST A LONG SHADOW

I can't believe our luck!

Aries and I came all this way to find the King who supposedly knows where Wind Walker is—and it turns out that Wind Walker *is* the King! I've got to say I'm pretty speechless right now. And since Aries and I risked our freedom entering the 13th Dimension to rescue Wind Walker in the first place, you'd think Aries would be whooping it up right now.

But instead, he's just standing there like a toy soldier, kidding around for me to bow before the King. I'll tell you, that guy's got one strange sense of humor.

"Funny, Aries," I say. "But seriously, now that we've found Wind Walker let's get out of here."

But Aries doesn't crack a smile.

What's wrong with him?

I'm about to ask Wind Walker if he knows what's up when I stop myself. As I stare into his narrow blue eyes, I realize something is off. But what?

Then it hits me.

Doesn't Wind Walker have green eyes?

Suddenly, blue electricity sparks from his pupils.

"Um, Wind Walker?" I say, my alarm bells ringing. "Are you okay?"

Instinctively, I take a step backward when the entrance to the chamber SLAMS shut behind me!

I'm trapped!

"Elliott Harkness," Wind Walker says, his voice a raspy whisper. "I have waited a long time for your arrival."

"Um, what?" I say, totally confused.

"I have exhausted every atom of my being to bring you here," Wind Walker continues. "I have pushed beyond inter-dimensional boundaries, reaching farther than my influence should allow. But now all of my labor bears fruit because you are here and the moment is upon us."

Well, that confirms it. Something is definitely wrong here. The Wind Walker I know doesn't talk like that. And he certainly wouldn't hold me against my will.

So, I figure I need to get out of here—and fast.

"Well, gee whiz," I say. "It's great seeing you too, but unfortunately I need to break up this little reunion. I just remembered I left my hairdryer plugged in and Dad hates it when I do that. So, if you could just open up the door for me, I promise I'll be back real soon."

"No," Wind Walker says. "You are not going anywhere. You are exactly where you are destined to be."

"Riiight," I say. "Listen, I appreciate that you went through hoops just to see me, but don't you think you're crossing the line between super-fan and stalker?"

"I have waited a long time for the arrival of someone with your power," Wind Walker says. "And this time I will not be tricked."

Tricked? What's he talking about?

And then the lightbulb goes off.

Maybe he's talking about Krule?

Maybe Krule somehow tricked him to escape from the 13th Dimension? But then it dawns on me, if this isn't the Wind Walker I know, who is he?

I mean, when the Overlord talked about the Wraiths, he referenced them in the plural, like there's more than one. But Wind Walker is talking in the first person, using words like 'I' and 'my.' So, what does that—

OMG!

My heart sinks to my toes.

Didn't that old woman tell us about something else that lived in the realm? Something that desperately wanted to escape. Something... evil?

I study my friend's face. He looks like Wind Walker, but his mind must have been taken over by... by...

"Holy smokes!" I blurt out. "You're not Wind Walker. You're the Shadow!"

"Indeed," the Shadow says. "But that is just one of my names. I am also known here as 'The Ruler,' or 'The Creator.' My power within this tiny realm is all-reaching. But in your larger realm, my voice is but the faintest of whispers. For between our realms there is a barrier I cannot break. So here I remain, limited in the scope of my power, barely sustaining myself on the energy of those trapped here."

Sustaining himself? On energy?

"Hang on," I say. "Are you saying you live off the Meta energy of others? Like... a vampire?"

"Meta energy is my sustenance," the Shadow says. "The origin of all of my power. But my food sources are limited here. When I finally escape to your realm, my food sources will be infinite. Then, I will rule over all realms, thanks to you."

"Thanks to me?" I say. "What do I have to do with your crazy plan?"

"Because you are rare," the Shadow says. "Only a few in the known multiverse possess the type of Meta energy that can release me from this prison."

"Um, sorry, but no way," I say.

He may be delusional, but I know he's right about one thing. I do have a unique kind of Meta power—Meta Manipulation. The only other Meta Manipulators I know are Meta-Taker and Siphon, but they're long gone. Could there really be others out there with this ability?

"You have no choice," the Shadow says. "Just as I am controlling the mouth of your friend, Wind Walker, I am also controlling his mind. And if you refuse to do my bidding, I will snuff it out like a candle. To prove my point, I will use your other friend for a quick demonstration of my power."

But before I can object, Aries' eyes flare with blue electricity and he begins walking towards me awkwardly, like a marionette on a string! I shuffle aside as he plows past me, only stopping when he slams face-first into the wall.

"Okay, okay," I say. "Calm down. I get it."

Well, that seals it. There's no freaking way I'm letting this monster out of the 13th Dimension. Somehow, I've got to get out of here with Wind Walker and Aries intact. But until I can figure that one out, I need to stall.

"Look, I'm listening," I say. "But first, tell me something. How could anyone trick someone as powerful as you?"

Wind Walker smiles.

"Even creators make mistakes," he says. "I was deceived. A new inhabitant entered the realm and I lured him here to my chamber where I could feed. But my mistake was in assuming he was weak and inept, just like all of the others."

Hold up! Is he saying he only sucks Meta energy here, in this chamber? Then, that would explain why

Aries could still use his powers above ground? We hadn't reached the Shadow's chamber yet, so Aries still had his powers the whole time!

And maybe I do too?

"But when he arrived," the Shadow continues, "I learned he was far from weak. His energy was strong, stronger than I had ever encountered before. And when I tried to feed upon him, he surprised me."

"Um, what does that mean?" I ask.

"Instead of taking possession of him," Wind Walker says, "he took possession of me. He bent my will and made me his slave. I could only watch as he used my All-Seeing Eye in ways I had never imagined. And then he escaped from the realm, leaving me behind."

The All-Seeing Eye? What's that?

And then the dots connect.

That giant purple crystal must be the All-Seeing Eye!

Krule must have used it to control the Time Trotter! And then Krule used it again to steal the Cosmic Key right out of Fairchild's hands! It all makes sense now!

But how did he actually project his powers through the crystal? I mean, I couldn't even get through to Dog-Gone.

"Listen," I say, "I get that Krule pulled a fast one on you, but what do you want from me? My powers are totally different than his."

"The manifestation of your powers may be different," he says, "but your energy is the same."

His comment shocks me.

Is he saying Krule is also a Meta Manipulator?

But then I realize something. Why hasn't the Shadow fed off of me? Does he think I'll take him over like Krule did? But I know I can't do that on my own.

I mean, Krule is some kind of a mega-Psychic. My powers don't work like that. But maybe the Shadow doesn't know that? Maybe I can bluff him?

"Sorry, but I still don't get it," I say, a bit more confidently. "What am I doing here?"

"Ever since I spotted you during your fateful encounter with Krule," he says, "I knew you were the one. You are not here by accident, Elliott Harkness. You are here by my grand design, with the help of some outside bargaining."

Huh? What does that mean?

"I see you are still confused," he says. "So, I will clarify things for you. Your arrest by the Paladins was no mistake. It was I who arranged for you to be taken to Paladin Planet."

What?

"Just as it was I who used Wind Walker's voice to cause your friend Aries' nightmares," he continues. "I planted the seed in Aries' mind to commit unspeakable crimes so he would end up on Paladin Planet, in the very cell next to you, only steps away from the entrance to the 13th Dimension."

"Whoa!" I say. "Slow down a sec. Are you telling me

you intentionally brought Aries and I to Paladin Planet at the same time? But why?"

"That is simple," he says. "I knew that once your trusted friend Aries informed you of Wind Walker's plight, you could not refuse to save him. Even if you had to travel into my realm—the dreaded 13th Dimension—to do so. That is how I brought you here. That is why you are standing before me now."

My mind is blown.

He used Wind Walker as bait to bring me here. I feel so... so... manipulated. But why?

"Okay," I say angrily. "Congratulations. You got me here. Now tell me what I'm doing here."

"That is simple," he says. "First, you will use the All-Seeing Eye to bring forth an image of the Cosmic Key. Then, you will use your abilities to reach through the crystal and duplicate its power, serving as my key to unlock the door and leave this realm forever."

"No way!" I yell.

"The choice is yours," he says. "You can either help me willingly, or I will take over your mind and do it myself, destroying your soul forever."

Meta Profile

Wind Walker

Name: Wohali Staar	Height: 6'1"
Race: Capachee	Weight: 215 lbs
Status: Hero/Active	Eyes/Hair: Green/Black

META 3: Energy Manipulator	Observed Characteristics	
Extreme Space Manipulation	Combat 90	
Generates wormholes that allow him to travel between worlds and across universes	Durability 45	Leadership 95
	Strategy 91	Willpower 99

ELEVEN

I WATCH MYSELF BACK AGAIN

They should really teach kids how to make life or death decisions in school.

I mean, the Shadow just basically gave me an ultimatum. Either I willingly use my powers to free him from the 13th Dimension, or he'll take over my body and do it anyway! Now that's a real problem, unlike those pesky algebra equations that never threaten to destroy anyone's soul. But then again, maybe they do.

"It is time," comes the Shadow's voice through Wind Walker's mouth. "What is your decision?"

"Oh, sorry," I say. "I was waiting for more choices. Are you saying there are no more choices?"

I can't keep stalling him. I've got to think fast.

I'm not exactly in a power position here.

Or am I?

I mean, maybe I'm not as powerless as I thought. As far as I know, he hasn't tried feeding off my Meta energy yet. Which means I may still have my powers.

I could try negating his power, but what if I mess up? The Shadow and Wind Walker are intertwined right now. If I cancel the Shadow's mind link with Wind Walker, would I accidentally cancel Wind Walker's brain functioning in the process? I've gotten a lot better at surgically targeting my powers, but I don't know if I'm that good. It's too risky.

But if I can't cancel his powers, I can always copy them. Maybe that would work? Then again, maybe I'm out of my mind.

Wait a second. That's it!

"Your time is up!" he demands. "Decide!"

"Okay, okay, take a chill pill," I say. "I've decided. Look, as much as I'd love to help fulfill your nutso fantasy of taking over the entire multiverse, I have a pretty strict policy of not working with bodiless parasites suffering from superiority complexes. So, I guess you'll just have to crush my soul. That is, if you can."

"What?" Wind Walker says, his eyebrows rising in surprise. "How dare you defy m—"

But I don't wait for him to stop yapping.

Instead, I go on the offensive.

I concentrate hard, washing my Meta energy over Wind Walker's body. Then, I replicate every iota of the

Shadow's power. Within milliseconds, I can feel his energy swirling inside my body.

Yes! My powers work!

But his energy feels so dark.

Heavy.

And I have an overwhelming sensation of... hunger.

A hunger for even more power.

Immediately, I can tell this was a bad idea.

The longer I hold on to this poisonous energy, the harder it's going to be to control. So, if I'm going to get the Shadow out of Wind Walker's mind, I've got to go in.

I focus all of the Shadow's power and then lash out, penetrating deep inside Wind Walker's mind.

There's a blinding white flash, and then everything goes topsy-turvy. The next thing I know, I'm standing on a clear platform surrounded by millions of gelatinous blobs floating all around me. Boy, Wind Walker's mind is a strange place.

What are those things?

Then, one of the blobs stops right in front of me, and my jaw drops, because inside the blob is the image of a village filled with blue-skinned people. Some are playing drums while others are dancing. It almost feels like a celebration. Then the image moves forward like I'm walking through the scene itself. The drums get louder and the dancers move aside, creating a pathway towards a teepee-like structure.

I push through the flaps of the teepee and enter.

Inside, a wrinkled old man wearing a headdress is sitting cross-legged on the ground.

"Wohali Starr," the man says, "it is time."

Wohali Starr?

Wait a minute, isn't that Wind Walker's real name?

"You have brought great pride to our people," the man continues. "But now it is time for you to leave us in the pursuit of everlasting peace. This is for you."

The man holds up a tan satchel with a shoulder strap. Hang on, I've seen that satchel before. Wind Walker wears it!

"No, Father," echoes a voice that sounds just like Wind Walker. "I am not worthy. The Spirit-catcher has belonged to the Chief of our tribe for generations. It is yours to use for the protection of our people."

And then I realize what's happening. I'm watching Wind Walker's memories through his very own eyes!

"There are none more worthy than you, my son," the man responds. "But you are mistaken. While it is true that the Spirit-catcher has been handed down for generations, it is not to be wielded by the Chief of our people, but by the greatest warrior of our people—and now that warrior is you. Use it with great care," he says, handing it to Wind Walker, "for it is ancient and powerful. Merely opening it will invite great danger."

Wind Walker takes the satchel in his hands. Interestingly, for something so ancient and powerful, it looks pretty ordinary.

"Wohali Starr," the old man continues, "the multiverse needs your courage and wisdom more than ever. I am proud of you, my son. Now go forth and discover your destiny."

Suddenly, the memory blobs shuffle and another scene presents itself. But this time I do a double take because I'm staring at an image of myself! I'm lying face down on the pavement in a place I know all too well—Keystone City! What's going on?

"Are you hurt?" comes Wind Walker's voice, again sounding like an echo.

"Just my pride," I watch myself mutter. "Don't worry, I'll be fine."

"Are you certain about this?" Wind Walker asks.

I cringe as I watch myself get up. It's kind of like seeing yourself in an awkward home movie. But where are we and why does this all seem so familiar?

"Very well," Wind Walker says. "Remember, you are no longer on your world. Places may appear identical, people may look familiar, but nothing is as it seems. For as long as you remain here, your greatest enemy is yourself. If you lower your guard, even for a second, it could cost you your life."

"Okay, okay," I say, smiling awkwardly. "I've got it. I can handle this."

"I hope so," Wind Walker says, "Now, I must try and solve the riddle of the Blur before it is too late. Good luck, Epic Zero. If you need me, call my name.

Hopefully, I will be able to return for you."

"Good luck," I say, as we shake hands.

"Do not forget what I told you," he says. Then, Wind Walker steps backward and is absorbed into one of his black voids.

OMG!

I know exactly what this is from. It's right after Wind Walker rescued me from the Rising Suns and brought me to Earth 2 in search of a second Orb of Oblivion.

But suddenly, the blob goes cloudy, and when it clears, I'm staring at Dog-Gone! That's weird. I don't remember Wind Walker ever meeting Dog-Gone?

"Good boy," Wind Walker says, scratching under Dog-Gone's chin. "There is somebody here who looks like your master but is not. At first, you may not trust him, but the two of you share a common goal — you are both searching for your master. So, remember, it is in your best interest to help him."

The next thing I know, I see myself running down the street to the Prop House. Then, it all comes flooding back. That's where Captain Justice 2 almost killed me! So that must be Dog-Gone 2!

"Follow that boy," Wind Walker says to Dog-Gone 2. "Protect him and keep him safe, at least until your mutual goal is achieved."

Dog-Gone 2 licks Wind Walker's hand and then runs after me, turning invisible after a few strides.

But what is this memory? I don't remember this.

And then it hits me!

Wind Walker didn't just leave me behind on Earth 2.

He must have found Dog-Gone 2 first and sent him to help me at the Prop House before he went looking for the Blur. He saved me from Captain Justice 2.

I-I never knew that.

But just as I'm processing that new info, the memory blobs rotate again and suddenly I'm staring at an image of an old woman sitting on a throne. But it's not just any old woman—it's the same old woman Aries and I met when we first entered the 13th Dimension!

And her eyes are sparking with blue electricity!

"Where am I?" Wind Walker asks.

"You poor unfortunate soul," the old woman says empathetically. "Why, you are in the realm. Now you must tell me how you got here. After all, you did not enter like the others."

"I-I do not know," Wind Walker answers. "I was tracking a great cosmic disturbance called the Blur, but for some reason when I tried cutting across this particular dimensional latitude, my worm-hole collapsed and I fell into this hidden pocket in space."

"Oh, I understand," the old woman says, nodding her head. "But tell me, do you know of a way out? Perhaps you can use those same powers that brought you here to get you out—to get us both out? Do you understand what I am asking? Do you think you can do that?"

"No," Wind Walker says. "I have tried, but I cannot. I seem to be trapped here."

Upon hearing Wind Walker's answer, the old woman's eyebrows furrow and her face turns a deep shade of red.

"Liar!" she screams. "I will not be deceived again! You will use your power to help me escape! You will help me escape at once!"

Then, her entire body dissipates into a black mist.

Huh? What's going on?

But before I can blink, she forms into the shape of a misty arrow and races straight towards us! I gasp, but right before impact, I snap back to reality.

Well, that was terrifying. At least now I know what happened to Wind Walker. No wonder he never responded to my calls. He got stuck here searching for the Blur. I bet he has no clue I solved that mystery when I defeated Ravager.

But more alarmingly, what's with that old woman? I knew there was something strange about her. But based on what I just saw, I think it's even worse. Because I think she may actually be the—

"Elliott Harkness," comes a woman's voice.

I spin around to find the old woman standing on the other side of the platform and I know I'm right.

"Elliott Harkness," she repeats, "you chose foolishly. And now I will crush your soul."

Yep, I was afraid of this.

The old woman and the Shadow aren't two different entities. They're one and the same!

The old woman *is* the Shadow!

But before I can react, she charges me, morphing into a black mist and blowing me backward with such force I land hard on my back! My body slides to the edge of the platform, my head hanging over. I look down and realize there's nothing below us!

If she knocks me off this thing, who knows where— or if—I'll ever land!

But before I can get up, she's on me again, pummeling me with blow after blow. I protect my head with my arms but it's no use. I don't know how to stop her! It's all I can do just to stay conscious!

Then, my brain feels like it's on fire!

OMG!

She's trying to get inside my head!

She weakened me physically so she can attack me mentally. But... I can't give up. I won't give up. I need to respond.

I muster all of the concentration I have left, drawing in all of my power. And then I form a mental barrier between us. If this doesn't work...

She pounds again, but this time I feel less of the blow. But she's relentless, pounding against me over and over again, trying to shatter my shield. I'm holding her back, but I won't be able to keep this up for long. I need a new strategy. I've got to get rid of her once and for all.

I close my eyes and build up my energy again.

I reach deep down inside.

Grabbing all of the dark energy.

I bundle it, squeezing it tight.

It's so powerful it's hard to contain it all.

But I keep it close. Scrunch it up like a ball.

Then, as soon as I feel her coming again, I close my eyes and release it.

There's an ear-piercing SCREAM.

And the pressure stops.

Did I do it?

Please, tell me I did it.

But to my surprise, when I open my eyes I find the old woman standing on the far side of the platform.

"You are powerful," she says. "But not as powerful as the one before you. Do not forget that you are in my realm, playing by my rules. And as I am one with the mind of your friend, Wind Walker, if you destroy me, I will ensure you destroy him as well!"

I swallow hard. That's what I was afraid of! That's why I didn't cancel her powers in the first place. I might turn Wind Walker into a vegetable! But if I don't do it, she'll destroy me!

"Yield!" she commands. "Or die!"

I-I don't know what to do!

"Erase her power," comes a faint but familiar voice.

What? Who is that?

"I believe in you, Epic Zero," the voice says. *"And even if*

you fail, being a slave to her wishes is no way to live."

Wait! I know that voice. It's-It's Wind Walker!

"Do it," he says. *"Erase her power."*

B-But I could screw up. I could...

"Please... for the sake of all... you must..."

Suddenly, I look up to find the old woman morphing into a whirlwind of black mist! She's swirling with such velocity she's scattering Wind Walker's memories all over the place. Then, she rears back and heads straight for me!

It's now or never!

Without a second thought, I fire all of my negation energy directly at the oncoming tornado, engulfing it, swallowing it whole.

But to my surprise, she keeps on coming! I lean forward and push harder, but so does she! Her force is so strong it knocks me backward towards the edge of the platform!

"Yield!" she cries.

"Go suck an egg!" I yell back.

But I don't understand why I can't negate her power.

Suddenly, she thrusts forward.

My left foot dangles over the edge.

She's too strong! I-I can't hold on!

"Enough!" comes a familiar voice.

And then, to my surprise, Wind Walker is standing between us, surrounded by a strange purplish glow.

"Shadow creature," Wind Walker says, "you have preyed upon the souls of others for far too long. Your reign of terror ends now."

Then, he raises his satchel—it's the Spirit-catcher!

But what's he doing with it?

"How did you escape my grasp?" the Shadow asks.

"Begone evil spirit!" Wind Walker commands, opening the flap. "Begone for all of eternity!"

Suddenly, I feel something pulling me in like I'm being sucked into a vacuum cleaner. I try holding back, but I'm losing my footing. Then, I see hundreds of Wind Walker's own memories flying into the satchel.

"Noooo!" the Shadow screams, as she's pulled inside, disappearing through the mouth of the satchel.

I grit my teeth and dig in, but the force is too strong, and the next thing I know, I'm airborne, flying straight towards the Spirit-catcher!

Meta Profile

The Shadow

Name: Unknown	Height: 5'2"
Race: Unknown	Weight: Unknown
Status: Spirit/Active	Eyes/Hair: Blue/White

Meta Power: Incalculable	Observed Characteristics	
A spirit entity	Combat +++	
Feeds off of Meta energy	Durability +++	Leadership +++
Holds immense Psychic power	Strategy +++	Willpower +++

TWELVE

I TAKE A RIDE

I'm flying headfirst into the Spirit-catcher!

As I hurtle towards the mouth of the mystical satchel, I can only watch in horror as more of Wind Walker's memories get sucked inside, followed by the last of the Shadow's misty tendrils!

Well, I guess that'll teach her.

But I'm next!

I stick out my arms, hoping to plug the opening like an oversized dust bunny, but I'm not sure it'll matter. Everything is getting sucked into the satchel, regardless of shape or size. I close my eyes.

What an undignified way to go.

Then, all of a sudden, the suction cuts off.

I crash to the floor like a bowling ball.

When I stop rolling, I realize I'm no longer inside Wind Walker's brain. In fact, I'm lying on the floor of the chamber at the foot of the throne—and above me sits Wind Walker!

I scramble to my feet, unsure of which Wind Walker I'm facing when I catch his eyes. They're back to green, his normal color! That's a good sign, until I realize he isn't moving. In fact, he isn't even blinking.

Then, I feel a tap on my shoulder.

"Epic Zero," Aries says, "are you okay?"

Aries? I step back and check out his eyes. They're back to their normal color too. And he's not moving around like a puppet anymore. He seems like his old self again.

"What happened?" he asks. "The last thing I remember is jumping inside that rock ring. After that, I don't remember anything. And what's wrong with Wind Walker? It's like he's in a trance."

"Well," I say. "It's a long story, but here's the quick version...."

As I run through the chain of events, I watch Aries' face fall. I tell him about the old woman being the Shadow, about Krule's escape using the All-Seeing Eye, and about the battle inside Wind Walker's mind. And then, of course, I explain how the Shadow manipulated Aries from afar. By the end of it all, he looks like he's going to be sick.

"Wow, seriously?" Aries says, rubbing his chin.

"That's crazy."

"I know," I say. "I'm sorry. But at least the Shadow is gone. But I'm not sure how long Wind Walker's satchel can hold her. She's really strong and she won't stay in there without a fight."

"I don't know," Aries says. "We'd have to ask Wind Walker about that. But he doesn't look like he's in any shape to answer."

"Wind Walker?" I say, shaking his shoulder.

But he doesn't respond. His chest is moving up and down so he's definitely breathing, but other than that, he's just staring straight ahead.

What's wrong with him?

But then I remember what happened.

"Oh no," I say. "When he opened his Spirit-catcher, he not only captured the Shadow, but most of his memories went in there as well. I-I think he accidentally erased a good portion of his own mind."

"What?" Aries says.

"We have to open the satchel!" I say. "It's the only way to fix him!"

"We can't do that," Aries says. "Knowing Wind Walker, this was no accident. He knew exactly what he was doing. He wouldn't want us to risk releasing the Shadow again for anything."

"But if we don't," I say, "he'll never be the same again. He'll be like this."

As I stare into Wind Walker's eyes, I'm totally

freaking out. I mean, did Wind Walker really do this on purpose? Did he really sacrifice his mind to prevent the Shadow from escaping?

"I know this is hard," Aries says, putting his hand on my shoulder. "But we both know there is no greater hero than Wind Walker. If he chose this course of action it must have been the only path he could take."

A tear slides down my cheek and I wipe it away.

I failed him. I mean, Wind Walker has always been there for me. Even in ways I didn't know of before today. And now he's like this because I couldn't defeat the Shadow on my own.

"Hey," Aries says. "It's okay. You did the best you could."

"Unfortunately, my best wasn't good enough," I say. "I don't even know what to do now."

"Now?" Aries says. "Now you'll take Wind Walker and go home."

"What?" I say shocked. "What do you mean? Aren't you coming?"

"No," Aries says, looking down. "My journey ends here. This is where I belong now."

"Are you crazy?" I ask. "What are you talking about? You can't stay here."

"I'm no longer a hero," Aries says. "My actions will haunt me for the rest of my life."

"You were being controlled by the Shadow!" I say. "You can't take responsibility for that. It's not fair."

"But I am the one responsible," Aries says. "Whether I was in control or not, my actions were mine and mine alone, and staying here will provide justice to the families of my victims. Plus, someone has to guard Wind Walker's Spirit-catcher. With the Shadow inside, we can't ever let it leave the 13th Dimension. Now, there's only one thing left to do."

"What's that?" I ask.

"Get you out of here," he says. "Maybe the Shadow was right about one thing. Maybe you can leave using the power of the All-Seeing Eye. Then, once you're gone, I'll destroy the crystal, preventing anyone from looking outside this dimension again."

***

A minute later, we're standing in front of the All-Seeing Eye. Aries is carrying Wind Walker, who still hasn't snapped back to normal, and honestly, I'm worried about him. I don't know if he'll ever recover from this.

The other person I'm worried about is Aries. Despite my arguments, I wasn't able to convince him to change his mind. I mean, I understand where he's coming from, but quite frankly I'm still shocked by his decision.

After all, who would want to stay in the 13th Dimension forever? But I guess that's the point. Being a hero means taking responsibility for your actions—no matter the consequences.

I look over at Aries and he nods.

Well, I guess this is it.

The last time I touched the crystal, I thought the images that popped up were random. But now I'm not so sure. Both Dog-Gone and Krule had been on my mind, so if I think hard enough, maybe I can get what I want to appear.

I press my palm against the surface and it changes from clear to opaque. Okay, I've got to focus. I close my eyes and fix an image in my mind, pushing away every unrelated thought. I concentrate on visualizing my goal, seeing it in my mind like it's right in front of my face. Then, when I think I have it good and nailed, I open my eyes, and there, floating before me, is a purple key.

The Cosmic Key!

I-I did it!

Now for the hard part. According to the Shadow, all I need to do is use my powers to reach through the crystal and copy the powers of the Cosmic Key. Never mind that it's in a totally different dimension. Well, this should be interesting.

I take a deep breath and try pushing my powers through the crystal itself, but I feel a wall of resistance. It's like my energy is spreading across the face of the crystal, not piercing through. This is hard, and beads of sweat form on my forehead. But I can't give up, this is our only ticket out of here.

Then, I remember the giant hammer Shaker turned

herself into. If I can smash through the barrier, then maybe I can reach the key. So, I gather my energy, pull it back, and then strike down with all of my might!

Suddenly, all resistance fades and my power pours through the crystal. It surrounds the Cosmic Key, latching on to it. Smothering it.

And then, I pull it back.

I feel a rush of power, like electricity.

My body feels like a live wire.

But it's so much power, I'm not going to be able to hold it for long. I'm going to have to let it go!

"Now!" I say.

"Hang on," Aries says, laying Wind Walker on the ground. The next thing I know he runs back into the chamber, and I hear a RIPPING sound. Seconds later he's back, balancing the gold throne on his palm like it's lighter than a feather. "We're going to need this."

Um, okay.

Then, he gently places Wind Walker onto the throne and picks up the chair. "Follow me," he says, bolting up the stairs at a ridiculous speed.

I do my best to keep up but it's not exactly easy climbing twelve flights of stairs while I'm trying to contain an unhealthy dose of cosmic energy. I mean, if I release it before we get to the top it'll all be for nothing!

By the time I reach the uppermost level my thighs are on fire and I bend over to catch my breath. That's when I notice Aries is holding some rope. He must have grabbed it from the third level. But before I can ask him what it's for, he jumps up and busts clear through the ceiling, opening the underground castle to the gray sky.

The light hits my eyes and I squint, just as Aries drops back in, grabs me, and takes me topside. As soon as we clear the hole, I feel a tremendous sense of relief.

Note to self: no more underground missions—ever!

But when my vision adjusts, I find Aries tying Wind Walker to the gold throne.

"What are you doing?" I ask.

"Securing him for your trip," he says, pulling the rope tight. "I'm guessing the only way out of the 13th Dimension is the way we came in."

What's he talking about? But as I follow his eyes, I remember how we got here. We fell into the 13th Dimension—from the freaking sky.

"Hold on," I say. "Are you, like, planning to throw us into the air?"

"Yep," he says. "This will test the limits of my Super-strength, but when you reach the edge of the atmosphere, the power of the Cosmic Key should unlock the barrier."

"Right," I say, "Great plan. But it's that word 'should' I'm worried about."

"Do you want to stay here forever?" he asks.

"Not really," I say.

"Then sit down in the chair," he says.

I hesitate, but I know he's right. This is my only way out of here, and my only shot to save Wind Walker.

"I can't believe I'm doing this," I say, sitting down next to Wind Walker.

Aries ties my body down, leaving my arms free. Then, I realize something.

"Wait," I say. "Do you have—"

"Wind Walker's satchel?" Aries says, holding it up. "Yes, I've got it right here."

"What are you going to do if the Shadow gets out?" I ask. "Not that I think she will. After all, she is kind of stuck inside a dimension stuffed inside another dimension. Kind of like a turducken."

"A tur-what?" he asks.

"A turducken," I say. "It's a chicken stuffed inside a duck that's stuffed inside a—oh, never mind. It's a silly Earth food invention. Don't ask why."

"I won't," Aries says with a smile. "Look, I promise I'll do whatever it takes to keep the Shadow here. Now let's work on getting you guys out of this place."

Aries picks up the throne.

"Do you have a good arm?" I ask.

"I think so," Aries says. "But I guess we'll find out. Ready?"

"Um, not really," I say.

"Great," he says. "Hold on."

I pull on the ropes to make sure we're tied down tight and they don't budge. Then, he rears back his massive arm.

OMG! This is going to happen! I close my eyes.

"Goodbye," Aries says. "Do good things when you get home."

But before I can respond, we're airborne, rocketing through the sky so fast I can barely catch my breath!

My heart is pumping and I feel a surge of power flare out of my body! Darn it! I don't know where this magic doorway is, but I can't blow all of the Cosmic Key's juice before we get there.

We're soaring higher and higher like we were shot out of a cannon. The wind is pressing hard against my face, blowing my hair back. But as we keep ascending, I can't help but wonder what'll happen when we finally reach our peak. After all, there is that little thing called 'gravity.' Man, that would stink.

Then, I see something out of the corner of my eye, moving between the clouds.

It's a black speck.

Nope, scratch that, it's a black speck—with wings!

And it's flying right for us!

Holy hamburger! It's the winged creature Aries and I saw earlier! Immediately, panic sets in. I mean, it looked big at ground level, but now that it's fast approaching, I can tell it's absolutely ginormous, with a huge snout and red eyes focused directly on me!

I look around but there's nowhere for us to go. We're sitting ducks tied to this chair! And why do I suddenly have the feeling this throne is slowing down? Meanwhile, the creature is only getting closer. It looks determined, flapping its monstrous wings harder and harder.

Then, I notice purple energy crackling all around me.

Uh no! I'm so freaked out I'm losing the power of the Cosmic Key! I can't control it! And when I look down, the beast has caught up with us!

It opens its mouth, revealing rows of sharp teeth!

This is not good!

I lean back and pull my feet up when—

BOOM!

The throne shakes violently.

THUD!

What was that?

I look down to see the creature's limp body shrinking in the distance as it freefalls towards the ground.

Huh? What happened?

Then, I realize we're no longer flying through gray clouds, but through a field of purple energy.

But that can only mean one thing.

We broke through the atmosphere!

We're heading out of the 13th Dimension!

I-I can't believe it! We did it!

Suddenly, there's a loud POP and our throne skids along a rough surface, generating sparks from the friction until we finally come to a stop. The ropes have come loose and I check on Wind Walker who miraculously is still breathing.

Ugh, for a second the world is spinning, and I feel

like I've been run over by a herd of elephants. In fact, I think I might hurl.

But that's fine with me because if we just accomplished what I think we accomplished, I'm going to celebrate like there's no—

"Elliott Harkness!" booms a familiar voice.

—tomorrow?

I roll over on my side to find a pair of fishy eyes staring down at me.

Oh no.

"Elliott Harkness," Quovaar repeats. "Welcome back to Paladin Planet. I am pleased to inform you that your trial will begin now."

THIRTEEN

I GO ON TRIAL

Talk about out of the frying pan and into the fire!

I mean, I just escaped from the freaking 13th Dimension, and now I'm sprawled out in front of the Interstellar Council and they want to start my trial right now!

And who says life isn't fair?

Normally this would be ridiculously traumatizing stuff. Especially because if I'm found guilty, I get a one-way ticket right back to the 13th Dimension. But I can't worry about me right now. I've got more important stuff to check on—like Wind Walker's health.

"Elliott Harkness," Quovaar says. "Perhaps you did not hear me. I said your trial begins now."

"I heard you," I say. "But before we start this ridiculous trial my friend needs medical attention. He's innocent in all of this. He's a hero named—"

"—Wind Walker," Quovaar says, finishing my sentence. "We are well aware of his deeds, as well as his mysterious disappearance. But what I do not understand is how he got inside the 13th Dimension."

"I'll give you all the gory details later," I say. "But right now, he needs help. He's not all here at the moment. He lost his memory helping me defeat the Shadow."

"The Intergalactic Paladins aid all heroes," Quovaar says, signaling to others with his staff. "But what is this 'Shadow' you speak of?"

Um, what?

"Sorry," I say, "but are you saying you've been sending criminals down there for who knows how long and you never knew there was a lunatic spirit lady in there who is trying to get out and conquer the entire multiverse?"

"We know not of what you speak," Quovaar says matter-of-factly. "And the Council demands that you reveal the whereabouts of your accomplice, Aries."

"He decided to stay behind," I say. "He believed that's where he needed to be."

"A wise decision," Quovaar says. "Perhaps you should have done the same."

Okay, now I've had just about enough of this guy. But I guess Xenox was right. There's no way I'll get a fair trial around here. I mean, he's practically convicting me before it even starts!

Suddenly, a bunch of Paladins drop from the sky. One brushes me back as the others tend to Wind Walker. After a few seconds, they use their Infinity Wands to create a stretcher and then cart Wind Walker away before I can even say goodbye.

I sure hope they can help him. I'm still amazed by what he did down there. I don't know many heroes who would knowingly erase their own memory to save the day—and that includes me.

"Now that we have addressed all distractions," Quovaar barks, "your trial shall commence!"

But then again, now might be a good time to start.

Quovaar moves to the center of the platform and bangs his staff on the floor three times. Suddenly, that jiggly guilt-monitor known as the Paladin's Pulse rises from behind the platform.

According to Quovaar, those globules will read the inner conscience of every Paladin present. They're all white now, but if the majority of them turn red by the end of my trial, I'm considered guilty-as-charged!

I don't know why they do it this way, but I do know one thing—I'll never eat Jello again.

As Quovaar takes his seat, I wonder what kind of damaging evidence they've gathered to use against me. Old report cards? A picture of my bowl cut from third grade? Whatever it is, I'm ready to get this show on the road. But shockingly, nothing happens.

I mean, what's going on? He said my trial was starting now. What are we waiting for, fireworks?

"Elliott Harkness," comes a voice from behind me.

I jump out of my skin.

Not cool.

I spin around to have a word with my surprise guest, but instead, I end up doing a double take. Because standing before me is a slender alien with blue, bug-like eyes and pink skin!

"Proog?" I say. "Is that really you?"

"No," the alien says. "As you well know, Proog is dead. My name is Broog. I am Proog's brother and the appointed prosecutor for your trial."

Wait, what? Proog's brother is my prosecutor? He's the one who will be trying to prove my guilt in front of everyone?

"Whoa, hang on," I say, addressing the Council. "This isn't fair. I mean, how can I possibly convince any of you that I'm innocent when I'm being tried by the brother of the deceased? I think that's called a… a 'conflict of interest?' They'd never allow that on Earth."

"Need I remind you that we are not on Earth," Quovaar says. "Here we govern by the—"

"—Order of the Paladin," I say, this time finishing his sentence. "Yada yada yada. Yeah, I get where this is going. You're setting me up. So, let me guess who is defending me, Krule the Conqueror?"

"I would advise you not to question our justice

system," Quovaar says. "Per the Order of the Paladin, you and you alone will bear the weight of defending your actions. The prosecution will be granted one witness, and you will be granted the same privilege."

One witness? OMG! I never decided on a witness!

"Speaking of witnesses, Honorable Council," Broog begins. "I would like to call forth my prime witness in this unfortunate case. Someone who has firsthand knowledge of the defendant's transgressions. Someone who was at the very scene of the crime."

At the scene of the crime? Who could that be?

"Bring forth your witness," Quovaar says.

"He is presently on his way," Broog says, gesturing towards the sky.

Looking up, I see four Paladins flying towards us, towing a box with their Infinity Wands. As the Paladins get closer, I study their faces, but I don't recognize any of them, so I'm not sure which one is the witness Broog was referring to.

But as they lower the box next to me, I take a step back. I was so focused on the Paladins I didn't register how large the box actually was. It's like ten feet tall and made out of tungsten steel!

What's that for?

Suddenly, the box shakes violently and I hear muffled noises coming from inside. That's when I realize something is in there!

"Open the cage," Broog commands.

Did he say 'cage?'

Just then, the front of the box lifts and my jaw drops, because standing inside is a ginormous, yellow-skinned man whose arms and legs are bound by chains!

It's... a Skelton?

The Paladins gasp, and at first, I think it's just some random Skelton warrior. But as I study his face more closely a chill runs down my spine, because I think I've seen him before. His eyes look familiar, except I don't remember all the wrinkles, or the white hairs sprouting from around his ears.

I'm racking my brain. How do I know him?

And then it hits me.

"Y-You're the Blood Master?" I stammer.

He looks at me with his neon green eyes and spits.

I-I can't believe it! The last time I saw him, he was working with Norman Fairchild to steal the Cosmic Key for the Skelton Empire. But that was thirty years ago when I traveled into the past.

And now he's... here?

"Honorable Council," Broog states. "I present my prime witness in these proceedings. His real name is Mowleg Grawl of Skelton, better known to all as the Blood Master. Of course, his reputation proceeds him. He is a natural-born killer and one of the top fugitives on the Intergalactic Paladin's Most Wanted List. Yet, he has been apprehended and I bring him before you because he has an important role to play in the case against Elliott

Harkness. Will you permit me to examine the witness?"

"Permission granted," Quovaar says.

"Thank you," Broog says with a slight bow. "Please tell us, Mowleg Grawl, do you know the defendant standing before you?"

The Blood Master sneers at me and says, "Yes."

"Excellent," Broog says. "You participated in the battle for the Cosmic Key at the institution known as ArmaTech on planet Earth. Is that correct?"

The Blood Master spits again, and then says, "Yes."

"Did the defendant participate as well?" Broog asks.

"Yes," he answers, his eyes never leaving mine.

"Please, Mowleg Grawl," Broog says, "It would be helpful if you could provide more than one-word answers."

"Then stop asking only one-word questions," the Blood Master says. "And I am called the Blood Master. I know of no other identity."

"Very well," Broog says. "Now tell us, Mow—I mean, Blood Master. What role do you remember the defendant playing at ArmaTech?"

"Before I say anything else," the Blood Master says, looking up at Quovaar, "I want assurances the deal for my freedom is still in place. Because I could break these chains in an instant if I wanted to."

Deal? Wait a minute. What deal?

"Silence, fool," Quovaar whispers through gritted teeth. "Now answer the question."

"I'll take that as a yes," the Blood Master says, looking my way. "Of course I remember him. I remember the whole situation like it was yesterday. That child goes by the name of Epic Zero. But at the battle itself, he was masquerading as a hero called the Nullifier. At first, I thought he was just another human weakling. But he proved me wrong."

"How so?" Broog asks, pacing back and forth. "What did the defendant do?"

"He destroyed an Infinity Wand," the Blood Master says. "I saw him do it."

There's murmuring in the audience.

"That's right," the Blood Master continues. "He sent a massive power surge into the Infinity Wand, shattering it into a gazillion pieces. That's what turned Norman Fairchild into the monster known as Meta-Taker."

The Paladins let out a collective gasp, then they start booing.

"Order!" Quovaar demands, tapping his staff against the floor. "Order, I say!"

The audience grows silent.

"So," Broog says, "you are claiming you witnessed the defendant intentionally destroy an Infinity Wand? Proog's Infinity Wand?"

"Yes," the Blood Master says.

"That's a lie!" I blurt out.

"Objection!" Broog yells. "It is not his turn."

"He couldn't have seen me," I say, ignoring him.

"He was unconscious at the time."

"Silence!" Quovaar orders, "your turn will come."

I look up at the Paladin's Pulse. Half the white globules have already turned red! This is not good!

"Go on," Broog says, nodding to his witness. "What else did you see?"

"What else?" the Blood Master says, taking a dramatic pause. "Oh, right. Well, then I saw him hand the Cosmic Key to Krule the Conqueror."

The crowd explodes.

What? But that's not true either!

"Honorable Council," Broog says. "I rest my case."

"Order!" Quovaar commands. "Order in the court!"

But the audience refuses to settle down.

Over the commotion, Quovaar looks at me and says, "Elliott Harkness, it is now time to hear from you. How do you plead to the serious charges brought against you and who will you call to testify as your witness?"

I-I want to declare my innocence.

But I did destroy an Infinity Wand.

And I don't have a witness.

I-I don't know what to do.

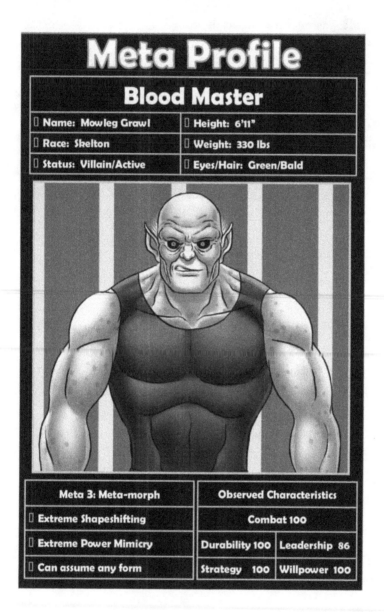

Meta Profile

Blood Master

Name: Mowleg Grawl	Height: 6'11"
Race: Skelton	Weight: 330 lbs
Status: Villain/Active	Eyes/Hair: Green/Bald

Meta 3: Meta-morph	Observed Characteristics	
Extreme Shapeshifting	Combat 100	
Extreme Power Mimicry	Durability 100	Leadership 86
Can assume any form	Strategy 100	Willpower 100

FOURTEEN

I MOUNT MY DEFENSE

All eyes are on me.

And I'm frozen!

I mean, this is my one chance to say everything I need to stay to stop this mockery of a trial from going any further. But the problem is, I'm the only one who knows the truth and no one else seems to care!

I try to collect myself, but it's clear everything is stacked up against me. I mean, my prosecutor is Proog's brother, his star witness is in cahoots with the Supreme Council, and nearly the entire Paladin's Pulse has turned red before the trial has even ended!

How can they not find me guilty?

"Elliott Harkness," Quovaar says, "please face the Supreme Council and tell us what you plead."

What do I plead? What can I plead?

For some reason, Aries crosses my mind. Even though he wasn't at fault, he sacrificed his freedom to give the families of his victims the justice they deserve. I don't think I've ever seen anyone step up to the plate like that before.

What should I say?

"Elliott Harkness," Quovaar repeats. "You are trying the patience of the Council. What do you plead and who will stand as your witness?"

I take a deep breath and exhale. All I can do is tell the truth and let the chips fall where they may.

"On the second count of aiding Krule's escape from the 13th Dimension," I say. "I plead not guilty."

There's a commotion in the stands.

"But on the first count of destroying an Infinity Wand," I say, yelling over the crowd. "I can only plead guilty—but I acted in self-defense."

The crowd erupts.

I glance at the Paladin's Pulse. It's all red.

The Paladins are eating this up—booing, hissing, and calling me nasty-sounding names in alien tongues I don't understand.

"Order!" Quovaar commands.

But the Paladins refuse to settle down.

"Drop him in!" cries a voice from the crowd.

"Send him to the 13th Dimension!" comes another.

I feel good about telling the truth. I'm just concerned it's not going to make a difference.

"Now who will you call as your witness?" Quovaar shouts over the crowd. "Order!" he commands, banging his staff on the platform.

But now I'm really in trouble because if I can't produce a witness credible enough to back up my side of the story, I'm toast. But who could I possibly call that could sway this biased audience?

"Order!" Quovaar demands again, this time rising to his feet. "Order in the court! I say order in the court!"

Wait. What did he just say?

Order…?

In the court?

That's it!

But it's a longshot.

And if it doesn't work, I'm doomed.

Finally, the Paladins settle down.

"Elliott Harkness," Quovaar says. "While you plead innocent to one charge, you plead guilty to the other, with a claim of self-defense. These accusations against you are serious, and this case must be carefully deliberated. Per the Order of the Paladin, you are allowed to call before the Court one witness who may try to support your claims. Once named, we will summon this individual to the Court immediately. Do you have such a witness?"

"Yes," I say, mustering as much confidence as I can. "I think I do have a witness."

"You do?" Quovaar says, his voice rising in surprise. "Very well then. Who is this so-called witness? Let us bring this individual before the Court at once."

"Certainly," I say. Then, I take a deep breath and say, "I call before the Court my witness. The one, the only, Order!"

I wave my arms with a flourish, waiting for his grand entrance. I'm expecting smoke, music, fireworks.

But embarrassingly, there's nothing.

Did I just make the biggest mistake of my life?

"Good evening, Elliott Harkness."

I jump out of my skin.

Standing behind me is a tall, purple-skinned man wearing a black suit with a white pocket square and tie.

"Order!" I say relieved. "You came?"

"Yes," he says. "I was not going to interfere in these proceedings, but the more I observed, the more I sensed my presence was required to ensure proper balance in the multiverse."

"Wh-Who are you?" Quovaar asks.

"I am Order," he says. "My purpose is to ensure structure, discipline, and boundaries in all things. And you are Quovaar, Supreme Justice of the Interstellar Council. An Interstellar Council that has presided for millennia based upon the principles of the Order of the Paladin— nobility, justice, and fairness. Yet, I sense an overwhelming darkness guiding these affairs."

"I know not of what you speak," Quovaar says.

"Perhaps not," Order says. "But this child is no mere criminal to be thrown to the wolves. He has proven himself a great hero. A great hero with a great destiny."

Um, what?

"He has been accused of serious crimes," Quovaar says. "He must stand trial."

"Must he?" Order says with a smirk. "Very well then. As I am his key witness, you must now observe."

Order snaps and a scene I recognize in my darkest nightmares repeats itself before everyone.

I'm back in ArmaTech. The Blood Master is lying unconscious on the floor, just as I remembered, while Fairchild and I are in a heated game of tug-of-war for the Cosmic Key.

"You are powerful," Fairchild says. "But not powerful enough."

Then, he points the Infinity Wand at a group of heroes, including Dynamo Joe and Blue Bolt. He zaps them with orange energy, and pulls it back into the Infinity Wand, absorbing their power.

"Now, it ends," Fairchild says, pointing the Infinity Wand at me! But the wand is shaking violently. It looks unstable.

Panic registers in my eyes as I focus all of my Meta energy and throw it at the Infinity Wand.

It causes a blinding explosion.

An explosion that created Meta-Taker.

"That is truly what happened that day," Order says. "Elliott Harkness did indeed destroy the Infinity Wand, but he did so to save himself and his colleagues from certain destruction. He acted the only way he knew how, like a true hero."

"B-But…" Quovaar stammers.

"Silence," Order says. "It is not your turn. Continue to observe."

The image shifts to me running at lightning speed towards Meta-Taker. The monster is holding the Cosmic Key, but just as I'm about to reach him a Pterodactyl swoops across the scene, biting the key right out of Meta-Taker's hand!

As Meta-Taker and I collide and tumble to the ground, the Pterodactyl disappears into a green vortex, taking the Cosmic Key with it!

"Finally," comes a booming voice from above.

And then, the face of Krule the Conqueror appears, gloating over us all. "The Cosmic Key is mine!" he says. "And now, the universe will be mine as well!"

Then, there's a flash of white light and he's gone.

"What do you think now?" Order asks. "Now that you have seen the truth?"

"I… I…" Quovaar mutters.

"This is a lie!" Broog states. "He is lying! That is not what happened! My brother did not die in vain!"

"No," Order says, putting his hand on Broog's shoulder. "Your brother did not die in vain. He died as a hero. But unfortunately, not all brothers are as heroic as yours."

"What do you mean?" Broog asks.

"I will answer your question shortly," Order says. "But first, let us put an end to this."

He snaps and Quovaar and Broog shake their heads.

"What happened?" Quovaar says. "What is going on here?"

"You have been manipulated," Order says.

"What?" Quovaar says. "By what?"

"The answer is not 'by what,'" Order says, looking to the sky. "But rather, 'by who.' Isn't that right, dear brother? I believe this trial has ended, but perhaps yours shall begin?"

Brother? Wait, does he mean—

Suddenly, another man appears next to Order. He looks just like him, but he's wearing sunglasses and a leather jacket!

"Chaos," Order says. "Have you had enough fun at the expense of these poor creatures?"

"Of course not," Chaos says. "But fun has a way of dying whenever you show up."

Chaos? What's he doing here?

Then it hits me.

Chaos must be responsible for all of this.

But why?

"What I do not understand is your motive," Order says. "Why choose this child? Has he not suffered enough?"

"You know me," Chaos says. "In the game of chess, it's always important to be a few moves ahead."

"I understand," Order says. "But there is more in store for this one, and the multiverse will need him."

"Your version of the multiverse needs him," Chaos says. "Not mine. I'll bargain anytime, anywhere, and with anyone for proper disorder."

Bargain? Wait a second. Didn't the Shadow mention she bargained with someone to get me into the 13th Dimension?

"You!" I blurt out. "You made a deal with the Shadow!"

"Yeah," Chaos says, buffing his nails. "I make millions of deals every second. Some work, some don't."

"I think it is time you departed," Order says. "And if you know what is good for you, I suggest you leave this one alone."

"Nah," Chaos says, winking at me. "Remember, he's one of your game pieces, not mine. Goodbye, brother. For now."

Then, he snaps and he's gone.

"Elliott Harkness," Quovaar says. "On behalf of the Intergalactic Paladins, I apologize for this gross abuse of power. We did not realize we were being manipulated. Of course, you are cleared of all charges from here to eternity."

I look over at the Paladin's Pulse and my eyes widen.

It's green!

The whole darn thing is green!

"Yes," Broog says, shaking my hand. "I must

apologize as well. In his final moments, I am sure my brother was thankful to have someone as brave as you by his side."

"He was the brave one," I say. "You would have been proud of him. He sacrificed everything to save the universe."

"Elliott Harkness," Order says. "You have been through a lot. Would you like me to return you home?"

Home? After all of this, I never thought I'd see home again. I mean, I know what I've gone through, but I can't even imagine how worried my parents must be.

But then I remember Wind Walker.

I can't just leave him like this.

"Do not worry," Order says with a smile, showing off his perfectly straight teeth. "I will take care of your friend for you. As my brother would say, he is one of my important game pieces as well."

"Really?" I say relieved. "That would be amazing."

"Very well," he says. "Shall we?"

"Yeah," I say.

"Goodbye, Elliott Harkness," Quovaar says. "We salute you. You are a true hero."

Suddenly, he raises his staff, emitting a bright orange light into the sky. And then, to my surprise, all of the Paladins follow suit, flickering their Infinity Wands in a brilliant display of unity.

I smile just as Order snaps.

And we're gone.

Meta Profile

Chaos

Name: Chaos	Height: Appears 7'0"
Race: Inapplicable	Weight: Unknown
Status: Cosmic Entity	Eyes/Hair: Unknown/White

Meta Power: Incalculable	Observed Characteristics	
Provides cosmic balance to his brother, Order	Combat +++	
Sole purpose is to create stress, disorder, and randomness in the universe	Durability +++	Leadership +++
	Strategy +++	Willpower +++

FIFTEEN

I TAKE THE STAGE

Water runs from a faucet as I stare at myself in a mirror.

No surprise, I look like a train wreck, but that doesn't matter right now. The only thing I want to know is where I am.

It doesn't take long to figure it out.

O.M.G.

I'm back in the bathroom at CNC headquarters!

Well, Order returned me home alright, but he dropped me off at the wrong location. I thought he was going to take me back to the Waystation. I'm bummed, but at least I'm not surrounded by Intergalactic Paladins.

Honestly, it feels strange being back here. I mean, the last time I was here I was making a fool of myself on live television. Who knows how much worse it could have been if I hadn't been abducted by those aliens?

Fortunately, I've probably been gone for days, so I'll never know the answer.

Well, there's no sense hiding in here any longer. I guess I'll head out and let the team know where they can pick me up. I can't wait to see Dog-Gone again, even though he owes me a new pair of slippers.

I turn off the faucet and reach for the door, when— KNOCK-KNOCK.

"Mr. Zero?" comes a woman's voice. "Mr. Zero, are you okay in there?"

I stop cold.

Wait a minute, I know that voice. It sounds like the woman who was wearing that headset.

But what's she still doing here?

"Mr. Zero?" she calls out again. "We really need you back on set. We're rolling live here. The second segment starts in less than a minute."

Second segment?

No. Freaking. Way!

If she's telling me my cruddy interview is still going on, then that means Order not only dropped me off at CNC, but he also returned me only seconds after I was taken by those Paladins!

I feel sick to my stomach.

Maybe I should go back to the 13th Dimension.

KNOCK-KNOCK.

"Mr. Zero?"

"Um, yeah," I respond. "Be right with you."

Holy horseshoes! I can't catch a break. This is totally the last thing I need right now. I don't want to go back out there. General Winch ate me alive!

I need to get out of here—and fast!

My eyes dart around the room looking for an escape route. Then, I notice a vent in the ceiling. Maybe I can pull myself up? No, it's too high. Then my eyes land on the toilet. Maybe I can escape through the sewer system?

It's messy, but it just might work!

But as I lift the lid, it dawns on me that this is crazy. First, I'll never fit down the drain, and second, if I got stuck and CNC got it on camera, my humiliation would live forever on Grace's screensaver.

So, I guess that only leaves one option.

Finish the interview.

KNOCK-KNOCK.

"Mr. Zero?"

I start pacing. I've got this, right? After all, didn't I just do the impossible? I mean, not just anyone could escape from the 13th Dimension or prove their innocence to a deluded court of Intergalactic Paladins. Compared to all of that, how bad could this be?

But then I remember that millions of people are watching me. I've already made a fool of myself once, so do I really want to do it again? Maybe I'll just tell them I'm not feeling well. Yeah, that's a good excuse.

But then I think of Aries and Wind Walker, and I feel guilty. They didn't make excuses. They did what needed to be done, no matter the personal consequences.

That's what real heroes do.

I rub my eyes. I know what I have to do, even if I don't want to do it. But I came here to do a job, so let's do the freaking job already.

I take a deep breath and exhale. Then, I open the door and march past a very relieved-looking woman.

"Are you okay?" she asks, running behind me.

"Golden," I say, entering the studio.

"Great," she says. "Here's your microphone."

As she attaches it to my collar, General Winch looks my way and flashes a condescending smile. I ignore him and take my seat.

"You okay, kid?" Sarah Anderson whispers.

"Yeah," I say. "I'm fine."

"Great," she says. "Now's your chance to take it to him. Ready?"

I nod and she turns to center camera. The man with the clipboard raises his hand and counts down from five with his fingers. Then, he gives us the thumbs up and the camera light turns on.

I swallow hard. We're live again.

"Welcome back to the CNC Morning Newsflash," Sarah Anderson begins. "We're ready for part two in our debate about Meta heroes—good guys or dangers to society. Joining us is General William Winch, former Chairman of the Joint Chiefs of Staff, and Epic Zebra, a young—"

"Excuse me, Ms. Anderson," I say. "But my name is not Epic Zebra. It's Epic Zero."

"What?" she says, looking down at her notes. "Oh, I'm so sorry. Please, forgive me for the unprofessional journalism, and don't worry, someone's head will roll for that. Well then, also joining us is Epic Zero, a young superhero partly responsible for yesterday's damage to the Keystone City subway system. Mr. Zero, let's start with you. Do Meta powers put the public at risk?"

I look straight at the camera, but this time I don't feel nearly as nervous. In fact, I'm feeling pretty good.

"I think the way you asked the question is important," I say. "But before we talk about Metas, let's talk about regular people. Would you say there are good people and bad people?"

"Well, yes," she says. "Of course."

"Exactly," I say. "Some people are good, but others are bad to the bone. And let's remember, any bad person who gets hold of a weapon can put the public at risk. So, having Meta powers isn't the problem. The problem comes when bad people have Meta powers. That's where Meta heroes come in. We stop Meta villains."

"That's a clever answer," General Winch says, "but it doesn't address the real problem. The real problem comes when some yahoo puts on a mask and thinks he's Captain Justice. Most of these so-called 'heroes' are untrained and risk people's lives and property. They're outlaws!"

He raises his chin, grinning like a Cheshire Cat. But

that won't be the end of this debate. Not on my watch.

"Tell me, General," I say calmly. "Without Meta heroes, who would have stopped Ravager from destroying our planet?"

"Well," he says. "The government, of course. We were prepared to detonate a nuclear bomb right into it."

"Really?" I say. "So, you're saying our government would have detonated a nuclear warhead right over the homes of its own citizens to stop an intergalactic monster with the consistency of a vapor cloud? Do you really think that would have worked, General?"

"Well," General Winch says, turning bright red. "That's not what our intelligence reports said at the time."

"Your intelligence reports were wrong," I say. "Just for the record, I traveled to another universe to find a proper solution to the Ravager problem."

"Wow, Mr. Zero," Sarah Anderson says. "That's truly impressive and I thank you for your work there. But if you don't mind, let's shift gears for a second because we have a special guest we'd like to bring into the conversation."

A special guest? Who could that be?

Suddenly, the screen behind us cuts to an image of a man with a handlebar mustache. For some reason, I feel like I know this guy, but it's not until I read his name and title that I remember who it is.

"This is Mr. Carl Frankel," Sarah Anderson says. "He

was the subway driver operating the L train who witnessed the events involving Mr. Zero firsthand. Welcome to the program, Mr. Frankel."

Oh no! The last time I saw him was seconds before I turned myself into sand to keep the train from derailing. I saved his life, but who knows what side he's on.

"Thank you, Ms. Anderson," he says. "It's a pleasure to be here."

"Mr. Frankel," she says, "you claim to have seen everything that happened down there. Can you tell us what you saw?"

I brace myself.

"Certainly," he says. "I saw what it means to be a hero. That boy right there saved my life and the lives of my passengers. If he wasn't there, I'm convinced those villains would have done something to my subway car and we'd be talking about multiple fatalities."

Wait, what? He's defending me?

"We're grateful you're unharmed, Mr. Frankel," she says. "But tell us, what if he wasn't there in the first place? What do you think would have happened then?"

"I have no doubt those villains still would have done something evil," Mr. Frankel says, "and we would have been defenseless against that kind of power. Listen, as the driver of a subway I've seen all kinds of people, and bad people are bad, whether they have Meta powers or not. I'm just thankful this boy was there and his actions saved a lot of lives that day. Thank you, Epic Zero, from the bottom of my heart."

"Gee," I say. "Thanks."

Then, the image of Mr. Frankel cuts out.

"Well, there you have it," Sarah Anderson says. "I guess the conclusion is that it's not the powers but the person that makes the difference, and we'll always need heroes to deal with the villains."

"Not true," General Winch says, pounding the desk. "Mark my words. Meta powers will be outlawed one day. One day soon."

Then, he stands up and leaves the stage.

"Okaaay," Sarah Anderson says. "Well, thank you, Mr. Zero, for sharing your perspective. It sounds like you are making a real difference in people's lives."

"Oh, no problem," I say. "But I'm not done yet. There's still something I need to do."

"Well, I can't wait to hear about it," she says. "But for now, that's it for the CNC Morning Newsflash. Be careful out there and have a terrific day."

"And cut!" the stagehand yells.

"Nice job, kid," Sarah Anderson says. "You came back strong. You really flustered the General."

"Yeah," I say. "I guess I did."

"Keep doing great things," she says. "And maybe we'll have you back."

"Um, thanks," I say, "but I've had enough of the limelight for a while."

"Fair enough," she says, shaking my hand. "Take

care, Epic Zero."

As she leaves, the woman with the headset takes my microphone and escorts me off the stage.

"Nice job, Mr. Zero," she says. "You handed it to that bully."

"Oh, thanks," I say. "It was nothing really."

As she leads me through a maze of hallways, I'm feeling pretty good about myself. I mean, believe me, I'm glad it's over, but I'm also happy I found my voice. It was a big responsibility to speak on behalf of my fellow heroes and I'm glad I didn't let them down.

Finally, we reach a doorway.

"Your family is right through here," she says.

"Thanks," I say, and as soon as I open the door, Dad wraps me up in a big hug.

"Way to go, champ!" he says. "You killed it!"

"Well," Grace says. "Truthfully, you were nearly killed. After the first part, I thought I'd have to give Dad CPR."

"Don't be silly, Grace," Dad says, shooting her a look. "He did a great job."

"Yeah," she says, hugging me. "You really did. I'm proud of you, bro."

"Thanks," I say.

"But what was that thing you said at the end?" Grace asks. "You said there's something you needed to do."

"Yep," I say. "And the good news is that you can do it with me."

Meta Profile

Order

Name: Order	Height: Appears 7'0"
Race: Inapplicable	Weight: Unknown
Status: Cosmic Entity	Eyes/Hair: Black/White

Meta Power: Incalculable	Observed Characteristics	
Provides cosmic balance to his brother, Chaos	Combat +++	
Sole purpose is to create structure, discipline, and boundaries in the universe	Durability +++	Leadership +++
	Strategy +++	Willpower +++

EPILOGUE

I GET BACK ON MY FEET

"This was a great idea, Elliott," Dad says.

"Thanks," I say, ensuring my goggles are secure as I drill the final nail into my stretch of subway track. "How's the third rail coming?"

"It's been replaced," Dad says, snapping in the wheel that carries power from the rail to the train's electric motor. "With 625 volts of electricity, I'd say I'm the right Meta to handle this job."

"For sure," I say. "How's the debris cleanup going?"

"It's all cleaned up," Mom says, "Between my telekinesis and Blue Bolt's speed, it didn't take long to remove it all."

"Excellent," I say. "And is the tunnel ceiling secure?"

"Just about," Grace says, floating above me. "TechnocRat is still inspecting our handiwork. After that, Master Mime can remove the energy beams holding the place up and we should be on our way. Hey, are you sure you don't want to get this on camera?" she says, fixing her hair. "I think I'm ready to get back in the spotlight."

"Um, no thanks," I say. "I'm not doing this for the publicity. Besides, I've had my fill of cameras."

Apparently, my interview with General Winch went viral. I saw some newsfeed article saying it broke all video streaming records, and there's been an overwhelming outpouring of support for Meta heroes, but honestly, that's not what it's about for me.

I realized that being a Meta doesn't make us better than anyone else. We're members of society too, and we need to take responsibility for our actions. Thankfully, the team agreed.

So, I was thrilled when Shadow Hawk got permission from the Keystone City Transit Authority allowing us to fix the subway line. It took all morning, but it saved Keystone City six months and millions of dollars.

"Well," Dad says, putting his hand on my shoulder, "I think we need to do more of this. I'm proud of you, son."

"Thanks," I say.

Suddenly, a rat with a jetpack drops down between us.

"Everything looks good," TechnocRat says. "This baby is approved to run."

"Great!" I say, pulling a walkie talkie out of my utility

belt. I push the button and speak into it. "Makeshift, we're good to go. Just give us a minute to get out of here and I'll give you the all-clear signal. Then you can tell the police to reopen the line."

There's static, and then an ear-piercing SQUAWK.

"Breaker 1-9," Makeshift says over the walkie talkie. "Mohawk numero uno responding. 10-4. Copy. Roger that. Affirmative. Over and out."

I roll my eyes. Who decided it was a good idea to give Makeshift a walkie talkie anyway?

"Okay," I announce, "let's roll!"

I start packing up my tools when I hear—

"Epic Zero."

I drop my drill and it CLANGS onto the track.

That voice? I'd know that voice anywhere!

It's Wind Walker!

I spin around to find him smiling at me, his green eyes looking alert. I throw my arms around him, squeezing him tight.

"You're okay?" I say, backing up, wiping tears from my cheeks. "I-I can't believe it."

"Epic Zero," Dad says, "who is this man?"

When I look up, the Freedom Force is standing all around us, ready for action.

"He's Wind Walker," I say. "The friend I told you about."

"I wanted to thank you," Wind Walker says. "You saved my life."

"Well, you saved mine," I say. "But wait… you remember?"

"Yes," he says. "My memories have returned. At least, most of them. But your actions were impossible to forget. I am forever indebted to you. And to Aries."

"Did you hear from him?" I ask, hopeful.

"Yes," Wind Walker says. "Order felt it was only fair to offer him the opportunity to leave the 13th Dimension, but Aries decided to stay. He said he had an important job to do making sure the Shadow stayed inside the Spirit-catcher, but he was happy we escaped."

I lower my head.

"I will never forget him either," Wind Walker says. "He demonstrated what it means to be a true hero. I will miss him greatly. But I have a gift for you."

"For me?" I say. "Really?"

"It is a small token," he says. "But when I was possessed by the Shadow, I became a part of her. Therefore, everything inside the realm became known to me, from the moment you entered to the moment you disconnected me from her power."

"Wow," I say. "Really?"

"Yes," he says. "I witnessed everything, including the images you saw through the All-Seeing Eye. Just as you observed Krule the Conqueror attacking the Skelton Homeworld, so did I."

OMG! With everything going on I completely forgot about Krule. But now it's all coming back to me.

"Since recovering, I have used my powers to secretly visit the Skelton Homeworld and I must report that Krule has completed his task," Wind Walker says. "He has conquered their planet. But that will not satisfy him for long. Eventually, he will try conquering more worlds, including this one."

"Boy," TechnocRat says, "that's some gift you've brought him. What are you gonna tell him next, there's a shortage on pizza?"

"I am sorry," Wind Walker says, "but this is a reality and you must be warned. But to respond to your comment, no, that is not my gift." Then, he unties a leather pouch from his belt and hands it to me. "This is for you. I recommend you do a better job of protecting these from your adversary. Be well, Epic Zero. And be aware. Always be aware."

Then, he winks at me and disappears!

"That was odd," Grace says. "What's in the pouch?"

"I don't know," I say.

I loosen the strings, reach inside, and feel two things that are soft with rubber bottoms. Wait a minute? No way! I pull them out and laugh.

Wow, I guess he really could see everything that happened in the 13th Dimension.

"Slippers?" Grace says. "He got you slippers?"

"Yep," I say, admiring them. They're the exact same pair as the ones Dog-Gone chewed up. "And they're absolutely perfect!"

EPIC ZERO 6 IS AVAILABLE NOW!

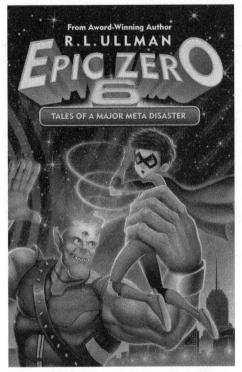

When Elliott fights a new law requiring Metas to turn themselves in, he discovers a sinister secret. The Skelton have infiltrated the highest ranks of government in a plan to take over the planet! But they aren't the only problem! Krule the Conqueror is heading straight for Earth, and Elliott may be the only one who can stop him!

Get Epic Zero 6:
Tales of a Major Meta Disaster today!

YOU CAN MAKE A BIG DIFFERENCE

Calling all heroes! I need your help to get Epic Zero 5 in front of more readers.

Reviews are extremely helpful in getting attention for my books. I wish I had the marketing muscle of the major publishers, but instead, I have something far more valuable, loyal readers, just like you! Your generosity in providing an honest review will help bring this book to the attention of more readers.

So, if you've enjoyed this book, I would be very grateful if you could spare a minute to leave a review on the book's Amazon page. Thanks for your support!

Stay Epic!

R.L. Ullman

META POWERS GLOSSARY

FROM THE META MONITOR:

There are nine known Meta power classifications. These classifications have been established to simplify Meta identification and provide a quick framework to understand a Meta's potential powers and capabilities. **Note:** Metas can possess powers in more than one classification. In addition, Metas can evolve over time in both the powers they express, as well as the effectiveness of their powers.

Due to the wide range of Meta abilities, superpowers have been further segmented into power levels. Power levels differ across Meta power classifications. In general, the following power levels have been established:

- Meta 0: Displays no Meta power.
- Meta 1: Displays limited Meta power.
- Meta 2: Displays considerable Meta power.
- Meta 3: Displays extreme Meta power.

The following is a brief overview of the nine Meta power classifications.

ENERGY MANIPULATION:

Energy Manipulation is the ability to generate, shape, or act as a conduit, for various forms of energy. Energy Manipulators can control energy by focusing or redirecting energy towards a specific target or shaping/reshaping energy for a specific task. Energy Manipulators are often impervious to the forms of energy they can manipulate.

Examples of the types of energies utilized by Energy Manipulators include, but are not limited to:

- Atomic
- Chemical
- Cosmic
- Electricity
- Gravity
- Heat
- Light
- Magnetic
- Sound
- Space
- Time

Note: the fundamental difference between an Energy Manipulator and a Meta-morph with Energy Manipulation capability is that an Energy Manipulator does not change their physical, molecular state to either generate or transfer energy (see META-MORPH).

FLIGHT:
Flight is the ability to fly, glide, or levitate above the Earth's surface without the use of an external source (e.g. jetpack). Flight can be accomplished through a variety of methods, these include, but are not limited to:

- Reversing the forces of gravity
- Riding air currents
- Using planetary magnetic fields
- Wings

Metas exhibiting Flight can range from barely sustaining flight a few feet off the ground to reaching the far limits of outer space.

Often, Metas with Flight ability also display the complementary ability of Super-Speed. However, it can be difficult to decipher if Super-Speed is a Meta power in its own right or is simply a function of combining the Meta's Flight ability with the Earth's natural gravitational force.

MAGIC:

Magic is the ability to display a wide variety of Meta abilities by channeling the powers of a secondary magical or mystical source. Known secondary sources of Magic powers include, but are not limited to:

- Alien lifeforms
- Dark arts
- Demonic forces
- Departed souls
- Mystical spirits

Typically, the forces of Magic are channeled through an enchanted object. Known magical, enchanted objects include:

- Amulets
- Books
- Cloaks
- Gemstones
- Wands

- Weapons

Some Magicians can transport themselves into the mystical realm of their magical source. They may also have the ability to transport others into and out of these realms as well.

Note: the fundamental difference between a Magician and an Energy Manipulator is that a Magician typically channels their powers from a mystical source that likely requires the use of an enchanted object to express these powers (see ENERGY MANIPULATOR).

META MANIPULATION:

Meta Manipulation is the ability to duplicate or negate the Meta powers of others. Meta Manipulation is a rare Meta power and can be extremely dangerous if the Meta Manipulator is capable of manipulating the powers of multiple Metas at one time. Meta Manipulators who can manipulate the powers of several Metas at once have been observed to reach Meta 4 power levels.

Based on the unique powers of the Meta Manipulator, it is hypothesized that other abilities could include altering or controlling the powers of others. Despite their tremendous abilities, Meta Manipulators are often unable to generate powers of their own and are limited to manipulating the powers of others. When not utilizing their abilities, Meta Manipulators may be vulnerable to attack.

Note: It has been observed that a Meta Manipulator requires close physical proximity to a Meta target to fully manipulate their power. When fighting a Meta

Manipulator, it is advised to stay at a reasonable distance and to attack from long range. Meta Manipulators have been observed manipulating the powers of others up to 100 yards away.

META-MORPH:

Meta-morph is the ability to display a wide variety of Meta abilities by "morphing" all, or part, of one's physical form from one state into another. There are two sub-types of Meta-morphs:

- Physical
- Molecular

Physical morphing occurs when a Meta-morph transforms their physical state to express their powers. Physical Meta-morphs typically maintain their human physiology while exhibiting their powers (with the exception of Shapeshifters). Types of Physical morphing include, but are not limited to:

- Invisibility
- Malleability (elasticity/plasticity)
- Physical by-products (silk, toxins, etc...)
- Shapeshifting
- Size changes (larger or smaller)

Molecular morphing occurs when a Meta-morph transforms their molecular state from a normal physical state to a non-physical state to express their powers. Types of Molecular morphing include, but are not limited to:

- Fire
- Ice
- Rock
- Sand
- Steel
- Water

Note: Because Meta-morphs can display abilities that mimic all other Meta power classifications, it can be difficult to properly identify a Meta-morph upon the first encounter. However, it is critical to carefully observe how their powers manifest, and, if it is through Physical or Molecular morphing, you can be certain you are dealing with a Meta-morph.

PSYCHIC:

Psychic is the ability to use one's mind as a weapon. There are two sub-types of Psychics:

- Telepaths
- Telekinetics

Telepathy is the ability to read and influence the thoughts of others. While Telepaths often do not appear to be physically intimidating, their power to penetrate minds can often result in more devastating damage than a physical assault.

Telekinesis is the ability to manipulate physical objects with one's mind. Telekinetics can often move objects with their mind that are much heavier than they could move physically. Many Telekinetics can also make objects move at very high speeds.

Note: Psychics are known to strike from long distance, and, in a fight, it is advised to incapacitate them as quickly as possible. Psychics often become physically drained from the extended use of their powers.

SUPER-INTELLIGENCE:

Super-Intelligence is the ability to display levels of intelligence above standard genius intellect. Super-Intelligence can manifest in many forms, including, but not limited to:

- Superior analytical ability
- Superior information synthesizing
- Superior learning capacity
- Superior reasoning skills

Note: Super-Intellects continuously push the envelope in the fields of technology, engineering, and weapons development. Super-Intellects are known to invent new approaches to accomplish previously impossible tasks. When dealing with a Super-Intellect, you should be mentally prepared to face challenges that have never been encountered before. In addition, Super-Intellects can come in all shapes and sizes. The most advanced Super-Intellects have originated from non-human creatures.

SUPER-SPEED:

Super-Speed is the ability to display movement at remarkable physical speeds above standard levels of speed. Metas with Super-Speed often exhibit complementary abilities to movement that include, but are not limited to:

- Enhanced endurance
- Phasing through solid objects
- Super-fast reflexes
- Time travel

Note: Metas with Super-Speed often have an equally super metabolism, burning thousands of calories per minute, and requiring them to eat many extra meals a day to maintain consistent energy levels. It has been observed that Metas exhibiting Super-Speed are quick thinkers, making it difficult to keep up with their thought process.

SUPER-STRENGTH:

Super-Strength is the ability to utilize muscles to display remarkable levels of physical strength above expected levels of strength. Metas with Super-Strength can lift or push objects that are well beyond the capability of an average member of their species. Metas exhibiting Super-Strength can range from lifting objects twice their weight to incalculable levels of strength allowing for the movement of planets.

Metas with Super-Strength often exhibit complementary abilities to strength that include, but are not limited to:

- Earthquake generation through stomping
- Enhanced jumping
- Invulnerability
- Shockwave generation through clapping

Note: Metas with Super-Strength may not always possess this strength evenly. Metas with Super-Strength have been observed to demonstrate powers in only one arm or leg.

META PROFILE CHARACTERISTICS

FROM THE META MONITOR:

In addition to having a strong working knowledge of a Meta's powers and capabilities, it is also imperative to understand the key characteristics that form the core of their character. When facing or teaming up with Metas, understanding their key characteristics will help you gain deeper insight into their mentality and strategic potential.

What follows is a brief explanation of the five key characteristics you should become familiar with. **Note**: the data that appears in each Meta profile has been compiled from live field activity.

COMBAT:

The ability to defeat a foe in hand-to-hand combat.

DURABILITY:

The ability to withstand significant wear, pressure, or damage.

LEADERSHIP:

The ability to lead a team of disparate personalities and powers to victory.

STRATEGY:

The ability to find, and successfully exploit, a foe's weakness.

WILLPOWER:

The ability to persevere despite seemingly insurmountable odds.

VISIT rlullman.com
FOR EVEN MORE EPIC FUN!

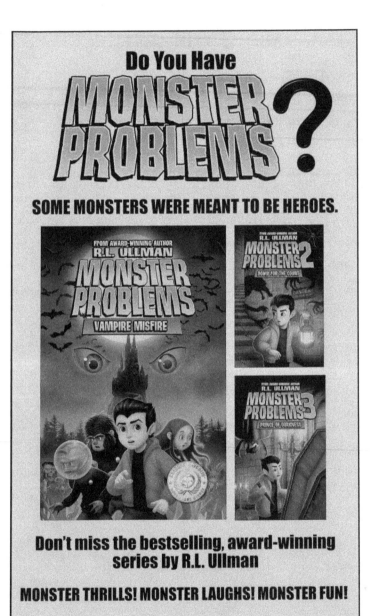

ABOUT THE AUTHOR

R.L. Ullman is the bestselling author of the award-winning EPIC ZERO series and the award-winning MONSTER PROBLEMS series. He creates fun, engaging page-turners that captivate the imaginations of kids and adults alike. His original, relatable characters face adventure and adversity that bring out their inner strengths. He's frequently distracted thinking up new stories, and once got lost in his own neighborhood. You can learn more about what R.L. is up to at rlullman.com, and if you see him wandering around your street please point him in the right direction home.

ACKNOWLEDGMENTS

Without the support of these brave heroes, I would have been trampled by supervillains before I could bring this series to print. I would like to thank my wife, Lynn (a.k.a. Mrs. Marvelous); my son Matthew (a.k.a. Captain Creativity); my daughter Olivia (a.k.a. Ms. Positivity); and my furry sidekicks Howie and Sadie. I would also like to thank all of the readers out there who have connected with Elliott and his amazing family. Stay Epic!

[183]

ABOUT THE AUTHOR

R.L. Ullman is the bestselling author of the award-winning EPIC ZERO series and the award-winning MONSTER PROBLEMS series. He creates fun, engaging page-turners that captivate the imaginations of kids and adults alike. His original, relatable characters face adventure and adversity that bring out their inner strengths. He's frequently distracted thinking up new stories, and once got lost in his own neighborhood. You can learn more about what R.L. is up to at rlullman.com, and if you see him wandering around your street please point him in the right direction home.

ACKNOWLEDGMENTS

Without the support of these brave heroes, I would have been trampled by supervillains before I could bring this series to print. I would like to thank my wife, Lynn (a.k.a. Mrs. Marvelous); my son Matthew (a.k.a. Captain Creativity); my daughter Olivia (a.k.a. Ms. Positivity); and my furry sidekicks Howie and Sadie. I would also like to thank all of the readers out there who have connected with Elliott and his amazing family. Stay Epic!

9 780998 412962